THE GOOSEBERRY FOOL

BOOKS BY JAMES MCCLURE

THE CATERPILLAR COP

THE STEAM PIG

THE BLOOD OF AN ENGLISHMAN

THE GOOSEBERRY FOOL

by

James McClure

Pantheon Books, New York

Reprint: Originally published by Harper & Row, New York, 1974.

The Library of Congress Cataloged the First Printing of this Title as Follows:

McClure, James, 1939—
   The gooseberry fool.
   I. Title.
PZ4.M12647Go   [PR9369.3.M3]   813'.5'4   73-14317
ISBN 0-394-71059-2

Manufactured in the United States of America

First Pantheon Paperback Edition

To Frances

The abbreviations used for government depart-
ments and agencies in this book are those offi-
cially recognized in the Republic of South
Africa. All characters are fictitious, although
the circumstances are founded on fact.

To play old gooseberry, to act as chap-
eron, play propriety, for a pair of lov-
ers; to make havoc.
The Oxford English Dictionary

THE GOOSEBERRY FOOL

one

Hugo Swart entered purgatory just after nine o'clock on the hottest night of the year. It came as a complete surprise to him, as it did to his several acquaintances, who, knowing him for a pious young bachelor, were unable to reconcile this with the thought of his brutal murder.

His surprise, however, was of a different order—owing nothing to assumption and everything to sudden agony as real as the improvised weapon with which it was inflicted. And in his final flare of consciousness, he acknowledged an inexplicable oversight.

This had been to presume that once inside his house, with the front door bolted and the back door locked, he was alone. He really should have considered the possibility of an intruder stealing in while he was away at Mass. Even just made the routine check carried out by any householder upon arrival home, let alone a man in his circumstances. Then he might have noticed a shadow flinch as he tossed his Missal across the darkened study onto his desk. But he did not. Nor did he actually go into the study, pausing only at the door.

Instead, with much that was pleasing on his mind, he went straight on through to the kitchen, humming to himself. His African servant had left the light burning in the ceiling and his dinner burning in the oven. The sharp smell of the ruined steak registered immediately, yet the only thought he gave to it was to switch off the stove. Thirst, rather than hunger, was his dominant drive.

He opened the refrigerator door and found everything he needed for a long, very cold drink. Vodka was his choice, for he believed it left the breath untainted—vodka and orange and plenty of ice. The simple procedure totally absorbed him. He measured out the spirit first, returning the bottle to its hiding place in the vegetable tray. Next came two fingers of fruit juice from a can, then three ice cubes, and finally a topping of chilled water. Instantly the tall glass frosted over and droplets began to wriggle down its thin sides. For it to be really cold, however, he had to wait until the ice did a little of its work.

So he turned on the radio over by the kettle and caught the news bulletin. December 23 had been the hottest day of the year, according to the South African Weather Bureau, which was not news to anyone. But they were right in making the heat wave the first item; there was an undeniable satisfaction in being part of the news oneself for a change, to know precisely how severe an ordeal it had been, to feel—however modestly—a survivor.

On every level, survival was dear to Hugo Swart, as it is to any man who anticipates a bright new future.

The idiot kettle began to boil. He thought at first that the sound, an odd wheeze, came from behind him, then noticed the air shimmering above the spout—it was altogether too hot and humid for steam to show. Of course. The kettle and the radio shared the same wall socket; switching them both on at once was a mistake he had made many times. And sure enough, after a moment's silence, the kettle gurgled and threatened to melt its element if more water was not swiftly added. That damn black baboon never left the thing properly filled. All it needed, though, was a sharp tug on the cord.

He gave it one and then took off his lightweight jacket, wishing he had done so ten minutes earlier, and dumped it on the drainboard.

By now the main news was over and the regional summary under way. It disclosed that the maximum temperature in Trekkersburg itself had soared to a record 112 degrees Fahrenheit.

"In the shade," the announcer added.

To which Hugo Swart, impatient with such pedantry, retorted aloud, "Jesus wept!"

His last words.

He dithered for a moment over his drink, then decided to increase the pleasure by prolonging the wait.

So he refilled the ice tray at the tap and put it back in the refrigerator. He closed the refrigerator door. He opened it and closed it again, musing. As children, he and his sister had once argued bitterly over whether the light in their stepmother's General Electric went out when the door was shut. The inspiration for this had been the claim of a fanciful friend who swore that a fairy, a sort of enslaved Jack Frost, lived on the inside, ready to douse the light the instant it was no longer needed. This was plainly a lot of rubbish, but posed a question nonetheless. He had held it was only logical that the light should go out, while his sister—who had sweets he wanted to share—perversely challenged him to prove it did not, in fact, stay on. Naturally, he was unable to do this, and ended up paying lip service to her irrational viewpoint. He knew that the light must go out, but it was as pointless an argument as that between an atheist and a priest debating the immortality of the soul: in both cases, nothing could be satisfactorily settled this side of the door.

Hugo Swart laughed softly. There was some truth in this talk of formative years. What he himself had learned was the practice of adopting whatever belief best served his own ends at any particular time. And it seemed to be working out very satisfactorily in this particular instance. Yes, sir.

His drink was ready. The ice cubes were half their size, and a wet ring was forming on the breakfast table. This had certainly been a moment worth waiting for, yet he decided on one further delay: a toast to his benefactors.

With the glass raised high, he turned to the window in the hope of seeing himself there in a comically cynical pose against the night. Unfortunately, the Venetian blinds were down and he could see nothing.

Even less than he supposed.

For, as he brought the lip of the glass to meet his own, somebody

3

struck him from behind with a steak knife. This first blow caught him on the left shoulder blade, skittered across the flat bone, and snagged between two vertebrae. Such was the violence of the blow, its force was transmitted to the extremities and the glass flew, untouched, from his hand. He saw it shatter and felt the terrible pain.

Strangely, he just stood there—hating the thought of waste, wondering what could conceivably be happening to him, noting that the next program would be a short interlude of chamber music. It startled him to finally realize there was someone else in the room, someone who wheezed when he breathed and must hate him very much.

That was his first surprise. There were others.

He staggered into a turn, grabbing at a fork that lay at the place set for his late supper. But he missed and never got to identify his assailant either. Before he could raise his reeling head, he was blind with his own blood—a wild slash with the knife having opened up the puffiness beneath his eyebrows.

On the cello's introductory note came the punched stab to the chest that knocked him back against the table. It was no good; all he could do was allow himself to sprawl onto the broken glass and try to think of something to say. Like Hail Mary.

Then, in the two beats of silence that followed, artfully contrived by the composer to key listeners for a bright gush of vital sound, Hugo Swart had his Adam's apple cored, and bled swiftly to death.

Lasting just long enough to hear his hearing aid being crushed underfoot—and then to reflect on what a fool he had been.

two

Lieutenant Tromp Kramer of the Trekkersburg Murder Squad sat alone in the third-floor lavatory and wondered if anyone would be giving him a birthday present. He was stark naked and held in his right hand a crumple of paper.

Man, it was hot. So hot it did things to the mind. His own had spent the day preoccupied with thoughts chill and sparkling and as far removed from homicide as a swimming pool from an acid bath. It had also evolved some extraordinary theories that had nothing to do with work either; such as a notion that the sun, having drawn up close, was watching, like a boy with a magnifying glass, its brightness burn holes in the map. If this was not the way it was, it was the way it felt—particularly in a hole like Trekkersburg. Right then he hated the skew hook behind the door and hated the back of his knees, which he found impossible to press against the cool porcelain pedestal.

The outer door squeaked open on its spring and slammed back. The tap at the basin was turned on and left to run in the vain hope its tepid flow would give way to cold water. Meanwhile, he of the sanguinary disposition performed an ashes-to-ashes routine with what sounded like a gallon of bleached Coke aimed at the wall.

Kramer frowned, displeased by this intrusion on his privacy. He determined not to invite any exchange, not as much as a hearty vulgarity by way of greeting, and remained very still. He was also careful to make no sound. Not even when knuckles rapped perfunctorily at about the height his clothes were hanging. Which was really a pity, because after the door had squeaked and slammed a second time, the lights were switched out.

Bugger. Now it was not only bloody hot but pitch bloody dark as well, and that put paid to the reading matter he had brought with him. He drew breath sharply. Another mistake, for it was like inhaling cheroot smoke on a dark night: dry, stifling, and nasty. Ah, well, this was where his self-indulgent little schemes usually landed him—right where he was perched. Back in his stuffy cupboard of an office, with its tease of a telephone and a queue of half-wits wanting their noses wiped, the idea of a trip down the passage had seemed a master stroke of contingency planning. For a full ten minutes before leaving his chair, he had savored the thought of stripping off and sitting undisturbed, emptying an occasional mugful from the cistern down his front when the mood took him. Yet another ten minutes later, it was plain this was not to be.

Bugger.

He stood up, bent over, pushed the paper between his lapels and into his jacket pocket, then began to dress. The absurdity of convention in such a climate, however temporarily extreme, was stressed once more as the warmth of his shirt, slacks, and socks, imperceptible on a winter's morning, engulfed him. His shoes, which had wandered off behind the brush container, seemed damp within and his toes enjoyed this. But his purple tie tightened like a tourniquet.

Done. The tedium of life—and death, for that matter—could begin again. With a pull on the chain for appearance' sake, an old habit he had never been able to kick, he unbolted the door and felt his way out into the passage—catching Colonel Muller with his finger on the light switch.

"Still here, Kramer?"

"Sir."

"Excitement too much for you, hey?"

"Always is, sir. But I'm on my way right now, never worry."

"Kramer."

"Sir?"

"You're the one with the worries. I'm off to the Free State over Christmas, and your old mate Colonel Du Plessis is taking charge."

Kramer mouthed a short word.

"Just what I had in mind," said the Colonel, grinning, as he disappeared through the door.

Like the good little Kaffir he was, Bantu Detective Sergeant Mickey Zondi had the Chevrolet waiting, its passenger door hanging open, right outside the main entrance to the CID building.

"You're bloody keen," grunted Kramer, sliding in beside him. How the hell Zondi managed to stay alive in that buttoned-up suit was more than he could imagine, wog or no wog. It must have been ten degrees hotter in there. Still, it did a lot for his image.

Zondi smiled, licking away a sting of saltiness from his upper lip. His expression was parboiled boredom, his face bright with sweat streaks. He started the engine, then teased the car against the hand brake. He needed directions.

"The note I had said the address was 40-something Sunderland Avenue," Kramer responded, digging into his jacket pocket. "No time to read it properly. That's right, 44."

It takes a lot to make tires screech on soft asphalt, but Zondi achieved this with a U-turn only he saw happen. In seconds, air was rushing in through the side vents so fast Kramer's eyeballs dried up.

He blinked casually and said, "I get the free funeral, you mad bastard. Remember that."

"Better," sighed Zondi, easing off for the traffic lights ahead. He stuck his right hand out of the window to funnel the false breeze up his sleeve.

"The note," Kramer began, his tone didactic, "the note says that the deceased is one Hugo Swart, aged thirty-three, a bachelor. He lived alone, worked for the provincial administration as a draftsman, and was a big churchgoer."

Zondi clicked his tongue.

"Multiple stab wounds—can mean anything. Last seen alive eight-thirty."

"By, boss?"

"By his priest, Father Lawrence, leaving the church. Same priest discovered the body when he came round about nine-thirty to discuss something or other. Steak knife; no fingerprints."

"Where was this body?"

"In the kitchen. Don't ask me how the priest got in. I don't know yet."

"Boss Swart was a *Catholic?* The Roman Danger?"

"Not everybody's Dutch Reformed who's got an Afrikaner name, man."

Zondi gave Kramer an impertinent sideways look and, fending the half punch neatly, took off on a show of green. His master was, at most, nonconforming agnostic.

"Any suspects, boss?"

"Local station say it must have been a Bantu intruder. They would; their bloody answer to everything. But I suppose they could be right. When last did anything really happen in this dump?"

"When the elephants lived here, I think."

"Too right. Stop if you see a tearoom that's open."

There was a late-night café a few blocks farther on, and Kramer had him buy them each an ice lollipop.

"I'll have the chocolate one," he said, when Zondi got back into the car. "Can't have you turning into a bloody cannibal or something."

These delicacies went down very well, lasting all the way out of the city, across the national road, and into the southern suburb of Skaapvlei. They ditched the sticks as Sunderland Avenue, lined by the ubiquitous jacaranda tree, twitched off to the left.

Just the name of the street would have been enough. Zondi had no need to check the house numbers; the address they sought was clearly indicated by an assortment of vehicles, ranging from the District Surgeon's Pontiac down to the mortuary van and two bicycles, parked haphazardly outside. There was also a crowd of servants on the far pavement, whispering and giggling behind cupped hands—and a few whites who had suddenly decided to walk the dog themselves. Things that only happen in films get all the extras they can use.

Before the Chevrolet had completely stopped, Kramer was out and

8

standing, thumbs hooked in hip pockets, looking the crowd over. He was careful how he did it, as somebody there might have something useful to say. Later on, that was. First he had to inspect the scene of the crime itself and get his bearings. So Kramer swiveled around to take in what the exterior of number 44 had to offer, nodding to Zondi to proceed as he did so.

The bungalow was the runt in a long line of handsome houses. Each of them had been born of a separate, conscious act of creation—of that blessed union between boom wealth and architectural talent which, because money is a dominant gene, invariably produces a brainchild as individual as its sire. That there were duplications of basic styles—Spanish colonial, early Cape Dutch, Californian aerodynamic, and restaurant Tudor—only went to show that nobody is quite the individual he believes himself to be. There was, however, nothing of the single-litter look of a speculator's estate about them, even where the bungalow was concerned. Doubtless its stunted growth had been the result of some nasty fright during gestation, perhaps a bull running wild in the stock exchange. Poor little sod, for it was plain that, had it risen another floor, then its roof would not have seemed so unnaturally large, nor its truncated Doric pilasters so stumpy. How out of place it must have felt, and yet quite unable to mix in any other company.

As a choice of abode, the bungalow was something else—unusual, to say the least, for a single man, and a humble civil servant at that. Kramer expected the first stirrings within him of interest in the case. None occurred.

He walked over to the other side of the road and stopped.

Instead there was this awareness that in some strange way he despised himself. Despised himself as he would a jaded Don Juan moving compulsively toward another whorehouse, another stranger's body, another act of professional intimacy, another striving to climax and release, all without feeling a thing. Not a damn thing. Just feeding a lust, then walking away again. Back past the loungers waiting outside, ready to grab you, eager to know what you knew and what you had done, too afraid to do it themselves, yet yearning. And how weary a bugger felt even before it began.

"Jesus, I need a holiday," he muttered, striding forward. Slowing down when he saw Sergeant Van der Poel, mincing, God help him, down the path with his right hand extended in greeting.

"That you, sir, Lieutenant?"

"It is, old mate."

"Thought so, sir. Knew you straightaway. Said to my constable that it was you who had arrived and it was."

Already the stupid bugger was finding a lot to say about nothing. Liked the sound of his own oily voice, did Van der Poel. Loved himself from cap to toecap, he did, which must have made his arse alone think it was something pretty special. Funny life for an arse that must be.

"Anything the matter, sir?"

There was: Kramer distrusted vain men. And vanity was all too apparent in the wavy locks slicked to cover a bald spot, in the uniform tailored to fit like a condom, in the Errol Flynn mustache trimmed to the brink of extinction above cupid's-bow lips.

"What's with your shoes, Van der Poel?"

"Pardon, sir?"

"You're walking like a bloody pimp."

How very satisfying this remark proved: it put things in perspective for both of them without wasted breath.

"This way, Lieutenant Kramer."

"Ta, old mate."

Inside the house, people were in every room and more especially the kitchen. Kramer ordered them all out with the exception of the priest, Father Lawrence, and the District Surgeon, Dr. Christiaan Strydom.

"Now we can get down to business," he said, crouching to inspect the corpse. The sequence of the wounds was self-evident, requiring no explanation from Strydom. First the stab in the back, then the follow-up in the chest, and the one in the throat. There was another, smaller cut above the eyes.

"Mixing himself a drink when some bloke got him from behind," he concluded.

"That's how I see it," Strydom concurred.

"Been here long?"

"I can be pretty sure about this one," Strydom replied. "His temp and other factors give us nine-fifteen as the time of death."

"I see. What time did you get here, Reverend?"

Father Lawrence looked up from his seat by the door.

For a man whose business was preparing for death, he was woefully unprepared for this one. His voice shook.

"I—I arrived at the house at nine-twenty, Lieutenant. I know this was ten minutes earlier than expected, but there are so few people to see in hospital at this time of year—Christmas, you know."

"I know," said Kramer.

"Sorry. Well, I didn't think—er—think Hugo would mind, and came up and knocked. I waited and no answer. We had an appointment at nine-thirty to make final arrangements for Midnight Mass. He was to have organized transport for our older parishioners living on their own, you know."

This time Kramer did not know but simply gave up.

"Then what?" coaxed Strydom gently.

"It was very odd, that's what I thought. Hugo always so punctual—and his car in the drive. I don't know why, but I gave the door a little push and it opened."

"Time, Reverend?"

"I must confess I didn't look at my watch, but only a minute or so had gone by. I called out and didn't get an answer. The radio was on; I could hear classical music of some kind. I called again, louder. Gave another knock. Hugo was, of course, extremely hard of hearing, Lieutenant."

"Deaf, you mean?"

"Very largely, but bore his cross with great courage. It's sad enough when you're born like that, but to have it happen to you in your prime is very different, much harder somehow."

"Oh, yes?" Strydom's professional interest was alerted.

"I can't tell you what sort of illness it was, doctor; an infection is all I remember. That's his hearing aid over there. Funny thing to smash, wasn't it, Lieutenant?"

"I've seen funnier, man, but that's probably why he didn't hear the killer coming up behind. I'll note it. Yes, so far this all makes sense."

Kramer moved crablike around to the other side of the body. He pointed to two rather odd, square-shaped lighter patches in the thickened blood.

"Doc?"

"Hadn't noticed those, to be honest."

"Ice," said Father Lawrence. "I wondered, too, but they hadn't quite melted when I got here."

"Uhuh, you've got a good eye, Reverend. Spot anything else?"

"No, nothing, Lieutenant."

"And you say he was at church earlier this evening?"

"We have Mass at seven-thirty and Holy Hour from eight. He was there all the time, in his usual pew on the side aisle, beyond the confessional."

"What's a Holy Hour, please?"

"A time for meditation, mainly. We pray individually and then at intervals together. Say the rosary. For the first half, though, I generally hear confessions."

"Do you get many folk at your Holy Hour then?"

Father Lawrence hesitated, anxious not to give the wrong impression.

"Enough of the faithful to make it worthwhile."

"How many's that?"

"Apart from the people at confession? About a dozen usually, I suppose."

"Just curiosity, you understand," Kramer said. "Now what can you tell me about Mr. Swart himself? How long has he been in this area? What were his plans?"

"I'm not sure I follow you, Lieutenant. Plans?"

"Well, a young man doesn't buy a house like this for nothing; that's what I mean."

"Oh, I see! Actually Hugo rented it; the landlord lives just round the corner—Mr. Potter, at 9 Osler Way."

"A big place for one."

"He was hoping to marry soon."

"Really? You know the girl?"

"No, she nurses in Cape Town. Her training ends in Easter and then Hugo and she . . ."

"Her name, Reverend? Someone will have to inform her if she's a fiancée."

"Judith Jugg—that's with two g's. I'm not sure which hospital, though. Perhaps a sanatorium, as she was also Cath—"

"Don't worry, we'll take care of that. So Mr. Swart was planning marriage and took this house. A bit expensive, shall we say?"

"I understand that Hugo managed to get it rather more cheaply than many houses round here. Mr. Potter and he were connected in some way. No good, I can't remember."

"Then I'll only ask you two more questions and you can go. Okay?"

Father Lawrence nodded. When all was said and done, he was an old man with gray hair, and exhaustion had now made his face gray, too. Had he been a grandfather, his children would have long since insisted on escorting him to his bed.

"Firstly, can you think of any reason why anyone should do this to Mr. Swart?"

"None at all. In the relatively short time I have known him, I have grown—grew to regard him as one of the finest lay Christians I have ever been graced to meet. Hugo was quiet, unassuming, yet always ready to lend a helping hand. He was also blessed with a quite outstanding ability to make the most of the power of prayer. Our Holy Hours took on . . ."

Father Lawrence was only just keeping himself from collapse. Strydom went over to his bag and rummaged for an appropriate pill. Kramer felt he had lived through the same scene once before.

"My other question, Reverend, then that's all," Kramer said. "Do you know if Mr. Swart ever partook of liquor?"

"It isn't against the laws of the Church, Lieutenant." Father Lawrence smiled faintly. "In fact, there's nothing I want more at this moment than a brandy in warm milk."

Then he concentrated again and shook his head.

"Hugo never touched a drop of alcohol," he added. "Nothing prudish, you understand; after all, our Lord drank wine. He never gave a reason but, well, I think it would have simply been out of keeping with his character, that's all. We still admired him for it, of course."

Kramer rose to shake hands and then Strydom accompanied the priest out to the street. On Strydom's return to the kitchen, he saw Kramer dip a finger in an orange-colored fluid splashed over the counter.

"Vodka," remarked Kramer, licking it.

"Then the plot thickens. Swart was mixing the drink for someone else —for a caller?"

"And the caller killed him for the bottle—because, if not, where has it got to? Not in any of the cupboards."

Strydom looked around and nodded.

"True, then the—"

"Then nothing." Kramer laughed, pulling out the vegetable tray and revealing the dead man's secret.

"I'll tell you something about our Mr. Swart here, doc: like most Catholics, he went to another church to say his confessions. That's a bet."

Strydom declined to put money on it; he had been caught more than once by the lieutenant.

"Not really any need for anyone to know," he ventured instead.

"Agreed. Let's you and me finish it off when we get back to your place. Got plenty of ice?"

"Destroy the evidence? Come, Lieutenant!"

"All in a good cause."

It was rare for Kramer to show any social inclinations. Strydom looked him over very carefully before replying.

"Agreed then. But first we both have some work left to do."

"True, doc. I haven't had a proper scratch round yet. Must be signs of a break-in somewhere, whatever Van der Poel says."

"And I'd better call in my lads and their meat tray. With the weather what it is, Mr. Swart here is long overdue in his freezer."

After a meticulous examination of all points of possible entry, Kramer had finally to admit to Van der Poel that he might be right. Nobody had forced his way into the house; either he had found a door or window open, or he had been in possession of a key.

"So I still say it was the servant boy—he had one," Van der Poel declared.

"Maybe, maybe not," Kramer replied, shrugging. "Your blokes haven't found him yet?"

"No, but they will. We've got his girl friend in the garage—your boy's talking to her."

"Zondi? We're all right then."

"Actually, sir, I was just going to ask if I—"

"Leave Kaffirs' work to Kaffirs, Van der Poel. Where did you grow up?"

Van der Poel had the surprising good sense to treat this as a joke, half of which it was. They walked in and out of a few more rooms in a desultory way and stopped once more in the study.

"Lot of books, sir."

"Maybe some dirty ones, too, if you look hard enough."

"Never!"

Kramer almost disclosed his discovery of the vodka but then saw no reason to share it with everyone. He was amused to see Van der Poel edge over to the shelves and cock his head sideways in search of a titillating title. If the man had any intelligence, he would look behind the big Bible.

"*Yirra*, this bloke must have been a professor," Van der Poel exclaimed, having reached the end of an incomprehensible row. "One hour on Sunday's enough for me—and that's not every Sunday, mind. Never turn down a Sunday duty if I get the chance."

"Hmmm? How's that?"

Kramer was not listening. He was taking a look through the desk and finding it about as exciting as frisking a store dummy. There were six drawers in all, five more than most people would have troubled to use for the meager contents. Bills, top left; receipts, top right; car papers, middle left; stationery, bottom right—and not as much as a puff of fluff or a loose pin to disrupt the arid orderliness. So he had to be wrong about the books—the dead man had not possessed enough passion to leave toothmarks on a bloody pencil.

"You're wrong about the books, sir."

"Uhuh."

"Find anything?"

"So-so. Swart lived within his means, kept most of his money in the bank, writing small checks for the day-to-day needs—in other words, I wouldn't say there's a cash box missing anywhere here. And I don't see how he'd have enough to buy anything worth stealing, so we can rule out the idea of theft."

"It's a good neighborhood, though, sir—housebreaker couldn't be expected to know what he had."

"Thought you said it was the servant?"

"I do—I mean . . ."

"You're crossing your wires, hey, Van der Poel? Take the ideas one at a time. Housebreaking: this place is a likely target because of its situation and because it's empty first part of most evenings, with Swart at church and the servant off duty. Say somehow a *skelm* got in here and was looking around when Swart got home. Now if Swart cornered him and then had been stabbed, I could understand it. But Swart was mixing himself a drink in the kitchen; all the housebreaker had to do was go out the front door. You can't tell me Swart was killed so that the *skelm* could finish looking; any damn fool could see straight off there was nothing here worth all this trouble."

A white constable knocked on the door and came in.

"Excuse me, Lieutenant, sir, but the sergeant is wanted on the telephone."

"Carry on, old mate," Kramer said, dismissing them both. Then he sat down behind the desk, found a place for his feet on the blotter, and went on uncrossing the wires in his own mind.

In the end, the only possible basis for the murder motive was something personal between Swart and his killer. *Personal,* that was it—a relationship that had gone lethally wrong. This made it murder proper, as opposed to a killing—a useful distinction which Kramer always sought to establish at the outset. Because murder itself had a pattern, and at least that was a start when, in a particular case, none other was immediately apparent. This pattern was basically statistical and concerned relationships. The exact figures were unimportant once you had absorbed their message, which came down to: you stood the least chance of being murdered by a work colleague, a greater chance of being murdered by a friend or close acquaintance, and the best chance of all of being murdered by a member of your household.

Now Father Lawrence had made it clear that Swart was both admired and liked at the church, and it was reasonable to suppose his behavior was equally unprovocative in the drafting office. The possibility certainly existed of his having friends and acquaintances outside these circles, but so far all the evidence pointed to a man far too disciplined for clandestine living. There was also the possibility, of course, that Swart, having committed a grievous wrong in his past, had become a penitent sinner only to finally pay the price when this wrong was secretly avenged. An attractive little theory in its way, but the sort apt to lead detection astray. The more obvious lines of inquiry had first to be explored.

Such as the statistical probability that the solution lay right there in the domestic situation. The priest had presumably told the truth, but history abounded with saints great and little who became fiends in the privacy of their own homes. Which was all well and good—except, with the girl friend so far away, the only relationship left was with the servant boy.

Kramer had now argued himself right back to where he had not wanted to finish up—on the same side of the table as Van der Poel. Inescapably, boringly, the wog was indeed the most likely candidate. To begin with, he had the wog mentality. Kramer did not ascribe to it a mystique capable of heinous crime totally without provocation, as Van der Poel undoubtedly did, but he conceded that here you had a thinking process—or rather, form of reaction—unlike his own. He had seen a word in English-language newspapers that described it well: overkill. And overkill there was in the shantytowns and alleyways of Trekkersburg —with the country as a whole, its population 22 million, racking up 6,500 murders a year. The only thing that made sense of it was to imagine that a small incident was the last straw on the camel's back. That inside every wog was this big sense of outrage and all you needed to do was add a touch more and the whole lot went up. What put it there in the first place was more than he had ever troubled to . . .

Bloody hell, this was sodding philosophy and he had a killer to catch! Correction, murderer.

The servant, then, may have been provoked beyond endurance by demands made upon him and have just struck out. Wait a moment, that burnt steak could have something to do with it. Swart comes home hot and tired, finds his supper spoiled, bawls for the servant, the servant comes in from his room in the yard, has it dropped on him from a dizzy height, Swart finishes what he has to say and turns his back—and gets it, with the first thing to hand: a steak knife. Then the servant backs out, locks the door, and runs for it. Good plausible stuff, however unoriginal. Originality in crime was something only whites seemed to think important anyway.

One reservation was all that he had: would Hugo Swart, the good Catholic, have staged such a scene with his employee? It was a good question, too, in days when the churches were troublemaking and telling their people to act soft like liberals. He would check with Zondi.

Kramer left the study, nodded to Van der Poel, who was still on the telephone in the hall, and went out to the garage. Only one side of the doorway was open, and there was not much light within, but he took in the details of the servant boy's girl friend without much difficulty.

She sat, fat and pathetic, on a fertilizer drum dragged out from a corner, holding her high-heeled shoes in one hand. She was sweating like everyone else that sweltering night, but giving off a very sweet sickliness, a by-product of cold fear. She shook. Trembled and gusted with long sighs. Rubbed tears into dimpled cheeks with the heel of the hand, making a proper mess. She wore a Salvation Army hat with the name ribbon sewn on upside down, and a cast-off frock that may have graced an administrator's reception—it had its own separate smell of salmon paste. She was terrified.

"Lucy Kwalumi," said Zondi, making the formal introductions. "Bantu female, works as cook girl at number 3 for Mr. and Mrs. Powell, says she is the wife of the boy here."

"What's his name, man?"

"Thomas Shabalala, sir. She says she has not seen him since when their off-time ended at four o'clock. She does not know where he is."

"You asked her about the off-time?"

"Yes, sir. She says she and Shabalala have their off-time two to four. Today they just sat on the pavement outside, talking."

"About?"

"She cannot remember. She says it was not important. There were others there, too. Along the gutter by where the car comes in."

"Did Shabalala talk about his master?"

"Not at all. He was a good master."

"Ask her if he ever shouted at Shabalala."

Zondi translated and then, after a sobbed reply that went on and on, interpreted.

"She says the master sometimes shouted—he was a master, wasn't he?"

"Bloody cheek."

"This one is not trying to be cheeky, boss."

"So he liked his master?"

Again Zondi translated and her nod saved time. Then Lucy suddenly volunteered some information on her own.

"It's all right, Zondi, I understand. Mr. Swart's churchgoing made things difficult in the evening?"

"That is true, sir. At first he made the boy wait on him nine, ten o'clock at night. He changed this after the priest made a joke about it when he ate at this place one time."

"So he wasn't such a good master then, hey?"

Lucy, who had not looked at Kramer while he was speaking in Afrikaans, jerked up her head as he switched to English.

"He was a good master because there was not much work," she replied in an amusing cultured English accent, giving away her employers as Home County far removed.

"I see; so he could be a lazy bugger if he wanted, is that it?"

Lucy giggled in obligatory fashion. Kramer, however, did not approve, and in a moment she was her unhappy self again. Zondi had a way with women—and with a spare fan belt, meaningfully slapped against the trouser leg.

19

"So you're his wife, you are?"

"Yes, boss."

"Are you barren?"

She did not answer.

"Kids—children. How many have you got?"

No reply.

"Ask her, Zondi."

So Zondi put the question into Zulu and she finally came up with the answer.

"She's barren."

"Thought so. You're just his town wife then? Hey? Come on, or there'll be trouble."

The wretched woman nodded once more, unable to conceal how deeply shamed she was by this admission.

"Where does his country wife live, Lucy?"

No reaction. Zondi moved in a step closer, having exchanged the fan belt for an insect spray with greater potential.

But Kramer surprised him.

"Outside, man," he said, walking out and down the drive a little way. Zondi followed, an eyebrow cocked.

"It's this way," Kramer explained. "Dr. Strydom and me have some other business to see to. I think I'll leave you here to see what Miss Lucy can tell us."

And then he outlined to Zondi his theory of how the attack in the kitchen had come about.

"Sounds good, boss. I have thought very much the same thing."

"So all you have to do is find out where the bugger's wife lives and you'll know where to pick him up. Only a proper *skelm* would know he must hide in the townships—he isn't one, is he?"

"No, an ordinary houseboy, boss. I'm sure of that."

"Don't let this Lucy have it too easy, though, Zondi. She probably knows something or she wouldn't have kept so quiet about being a town wife."

"I do not agree, boss. It was just she did not like to say she cannot have babies. There is much shame in this for a Zulu woman. It is also a bad life—a town wife is not high up like country wife."

"Town whore, more like."

"Not this one, boss. She has been with just Shabalala all the time he works in this road."

"Then I'll leave it to you to decide. Don't make a mistake, though, or I'll hang you up by your bloody tail. Okay?"

"Okay," Zondi replied, pleased to be entrusted with a free hand. "But what about Sergeant Van der Poel?"

"I'll speak to him, never fear. Oh, and I'll leave the Chev for you— I'll go with the doctor in his car."

Zondi would have thanked him but at that moment they became aware that Van der Poel had come up to them, so instead he gave a sulky shrug and shuffled off back to the garage.

"Doesn't want to be left alone then, Lieutenant? Like bloody children they are, always wanting you to help them."

"True, and a man can't be in two places at once," Kramer replied lightly. "At this stage, this is more his line than ours. A Bantu job."

"The servant Shabalala?"

"Maybe, old mate—you could be right after all."

This was less than generous of Kramer—he was 99 percent sure Shabalala had run amok—but it delighted Van der Poel just the same, worst luck.

"Thank you, sir! You'll—er—maybe mention it in your . . .?"

"Naturally."

"Do you want me to start a hunt for the boy right away?"

"Waste of manpower. Best we give him time to get back to his hut and pick him up there tomorrow. If we start looking tonight, that means anything up to two hundred miles of road and bush."

"Trains, sir?"

"The Railway Police wouldn't thank you."

Van der Poel, robbed of showing his initiative, took it hard.

"What do you want me to do then, sir?"

"Just keep a couple of Bantu constables guarding the property, then get along home—you were on a two-to-ten, weren't you?"

"Yes, sir. Your boy will be all right here by himself?"

"He'd better be. I've already told him what will happen if anything goes wrong."

Van der Poel sniggered silently. Then he remembered what had brought him out into the garden.

"Doc Strydom's going to a crash, sir," he said. "He says you've got to go with him."

The cunning old devil! He must have built up quite a thirst by now, and was eager to have their secret out and open.

"Me?" protested Kramer, as he felt he ought to do. "Christ, I thought I'd had enough of routine cases for one night!"

And, without knowing it, brought comfort to an ear not five yards away in the shadows.

three

Dr. Strydom drove well, if faster than Kramer had anticipated. They crossed the national road and headed north into the center of Trekkersburg, along streets almost empty of traffic. It was after midnight, long after curfew, and so the only pedestrians were white and few in number. It was also still very hot.

"Where's the booze?" Kramer asked.

Strydom jerked his thumb over his shoulder. Kramer looked and saw the black medicine bag on the back seat—the perfect thing for removing such an exhibit.

"Great," said Kramer.

"Must say I was surprised when you suggested a get-together, Lieutenant. Always regarded you as a bit of a lone wolf."

"Long as you aren't Red Riding Hood, you're okay, doc."

Strydom would have laughed but was not too sure of Kramer's tone. Then a quick sideways glance reassured him that his passenger was very relaxed and good-humored.

"The truth is," said Kramer, "I just don't give a bugger tonight somehow. Or all week, for that matter. Year, if you like."

"Nonsense, man. You did a fine job on that case up in Ladysmith. Who else would have thought of looking for the revolver in the Siege Museum? Bet I could take a guess at what the trouble is, Lieutenant."

"I should take a holiday?"

"No, not the heat either. I hear the—"

Then he thought better of it, which was just as well, for Kramer would never tolerate his private life being discussed, particularly if curiosity rather than compassion prompted the questions. Strydom was not the only snoopy bastard who had tried to find out what the Widow Fourie was doing in the Cape.

"Hear what, doc? That the Colonel is away in the Free State?"

"Yes, that's it; you two work well together," Strydom replied, grateful for a small mercy.

Which put a natural end to their conversation for a while. Finally, however, Strydom became uncomfortable in the silence.

"What are you thinking?" he ventured.

"That this is a bloody long way round to your place. You've moved or something?"

"Work before play, Lieutenant."

"What—you've got another job?"

"And so have you. Didn't Van der Poel tell you?"

"Hey?"

"There's been a car crash up on Turner's Hill that Traffic aren't too happy about. That's why they said you were to go along, too."

"*They?* Colonel Du Plessis?"

"That's what they told Van der Poel."

"Jesus."

"Didn't you know?"

Kramer had been told, of course he had, but not for a moment— This was the bloody end. The bloody sodding bloody end. A *car crash*, for God's sake! They'd have him out checking on passes next. It did not make sense. Not at all. Not in a thousand years. Never. Then it did. It made sense the way the unfamiliar sound of a silencer makes sense when the slug slams in above your head.

Some bastard was out to get him, and that bastard just had to be Colonel Granny Bloody Du Plessis. The old bitch had never forgiven Kramer for making a fool of him in the Le Roux case, nor Colonel Muller for having taken his place when he was pushed sideways out of

24

CID. But now that he was back at the helm over Christmas and set on having himself some fun, no doubt he would find a few willing helpers —snivelers who had been trouble since they messed their first diapers. Trouble and stealth and quick smiles and just enough brain to know which way was up and how to creep an arse to get there. This was of course a chance they, too, had been waiting for. Bastards like Viljoen and Prinsloo and Evans and Van Reenen and . . . If the list had been any shorter, he would have picked them off long ago, round behind the lockup where the wogs could enjoy the squeals. Which was not quite true, for normally he never gave them a second thought, and there would always be others. More inadequates, more incompetents, jealous of his work, calling it luck, finding comfort in sharp little whispers, pinpricks like mad old women made in wax models, expecting him to wither away. Now, however, he was obliged to give them some thought, for he was under orders and had to obey them. *Them!* Christ, but that's what it amounted to. Obey their orders or get out. If he quit, Colonel Muller would have lost a point, too. If he disobeyed orders, the same thing. Screw them. He would stick with it and find a way of obeying orders that would make a lasting impression. Dear God, yes. The bastards.

"What aren't they happy about, doc?" Kramer's voice growled, giving away his frame of mind. He quickly added with a chuckle, "Not that car crashes are meant to make you happy, in the first place."

Another quick sideways glance from Strydom.

"To be honest, I don't know, Lieutenant. We'll be able to see for ourselves over this rise."

His headlights dipped down a long straight road into a sharp right-hand bend. This bend was so dangerous there were no less than three signs warning drivers of what lay ahead, even though it was perfectly clear that gear changes and caution were imperative. At the bottom of the hill were a pile of wreckage and a small crowd. Somebody had gone right through the safety rails.

"A right maniac, this one," Strydom murmured, finding a place to park. "First pileup there's been on Turner's Hill since the signs went up."

Kramer climbed out and stretched, playing it all very cool. The Traffic sergeant in charge scrambled up the bank and saluted him. Kramer ignored him, walked on down the road, taking in the scene. The sergeant tagged along, embarrassed, looking for support from Strydom and getting none.

"No skid marks," said Kramer. "But the brakes are working."

The sergeant was decidedly impressed.

"Yes, sir!"

"And the steering is working."

"Right, sir!"

"And the gears are okay, too."

"Sir!"

"Why didn't the silly bugger make the corner? Is that the question?"

"I'd say he didn't want to, sir—he was wanting to kill himself."

"Is this unusual?"

"No, sir. We come across it but it's always hard to say. Often we're sure but . . ."

"I read in a magazine," said Kramer, "that they think suicides are becoming more common using cars."

"What I mean, sir."

"So? Why send for me? You know all the answers."

"I didn't send, sir. I was told you were coming."

Kramer thought about this for a moment, then went over to the sergeant's car. He reached in and lifted the radio handpiece.

"Give me CID Control," he said. "I want to talk to Colonel Du Plessis."

After a wait of three minutes, Kramer was informed that the Colonel had long since left the building but the duty officer, Captain Malan, was ready to speak to him. Malan was a white man in both meanings of the word.

"Trompie?"

"Koos, maybe you can tell me what the hell I'm doing out here at this fatal. The sergeant has the situation under control and I've got other problems, man."

"Hell, I wish I knew, Trompie."

"It's your bloody job, isn't it?"

26

"All I have is what Colonel Du Plessis said before he went. He wants you to take a very careful look at that crash—a full investigation."

"And that's all?"

"All I have."

"He knows I've got a murder?"

"Says it's in good hands."

"Zondi? That will be the day!"

"What he said."

"Okay, but I'm still the investigating officer—does he realize?"

"I suppose so, Trompie. Look, man, I'm sorry I can't tell you more. Maybe the bloke in that car has a big life insurance."

"Not my job to help insurance companies, Koos."

"Suicide's a crime."

"Uhuh. Capital offense, too, I hear. Be seeing you."

Kramer replaced the handpiece and lit his first cigarette in twelve—no, eighteen—hours. The tobacco tasted like grass from under a lamppost.

"Chucking them up?" joked Strydom, ducking as it arced into the night. There were times when his sense of humor, juxtaposed with a mangled being, gave some the idea he was an aging ghoul.

"What's new?" Kramer asked, taking out his notebook.

"No need, Lieutenant. You'll get my report tomorrow morning."

"By the book," Kramer replied, getting a glimmer of how he was going to have a lot of pleasure taking orders.

"Off the record," Strydom insisted. "I'm too damn tired to be precise tonight. The driver of that thing is deader than anything I've seen in a long time."

"Oh, yes?"

"Decapitated."

"Uhuh."

"And telescoped."

"How's that?"

"Must have been standing on the floorboards when he hit, arching his body back against the seat. Thigh bones right up into his trunk."

"Arms?"

"That's the strange thing. Must have taken both hands off the wheel before impact because—"

"I believe you. Drink?"

"Yes, a definite smell of it. No bottles in the car, though. A lot of blood."

"I bet."

"We've seen our fair share of it tonight, Lieutenant. Is there any point in staying on here?"

"Can't have been vodka," Kramer said with a slight smile. "Not if you could smell it."

As it turned out, the pilfered vodka did little for either of them. Exhaustion had Strydom snoring halfway through his first glass, and Kramer, who drank seldom and then never alone, lost interest after his second. The ice was welcome, though, and he crunched away at it as he pondered his next move.

Perhaps he ought to have remained at the accident and supervised the sergeant's tape measurings. But he really did not feel this was necessary —and had lost much of his determination to give the incident the full treatment. By doing so, he could well embarrass Colonel Du Plessis, but the cost was high. Perhaps, by the morning, he would have another plan.

It *was* the morning, damn it. Four o'clock by the cuckoo clock unless the bird had the burps. No, four it was, and his mind beginning to slow down. It was also much cooler and a faint breeze was rattling the dry leaves on palm trees outside the window. Death-rattling them at an hour when, they said, the old passed away in their sleep. Sometimes he forgot there were folk like that, people who died peacefully in their own beds, just buggered off without a fuss. . . .

Zondi. He would have to know what was in the wind, for Du Plessis had shown his dislike for the Kaffir before, and not in a nice way.

Kramer reached for the telephone, then thought better of it; Van der Poel could still be hanging about, all ears and tittle-tattle. So he rose, lifted Strydom like a sleeping child, and carried him through to the bedroom. Ma Strydom murmured an endearment as her spouse's weight sagged the big bed, then rolled over with her face to the wall. And she stayed asleep while he was manhandled in under the single light covering.

Before he left the room, Kramer paused in the doorway, looking back. It had never occurred to him that someday he might strip old Strydom naked and slip him beneath a sheet. The idea was amusing—but not quite as jolly as the thought of what the doc, whose pajamas were still under the pillow, would offer as an explanation in the morning.

A false dawn was in the sky as Kramer finally reached the turnoff to Sunderland Avenue. He had had to walk back to his place to pick up his own private Ford, and then call at an all-night filling station for petrol.

Thank God the Chev was still parked outside number 44, for it meant Zondi was still there. Van der Poel's Land-Rover had gone, another relief, and so had all the other vehicles, with the exception of the two bicycles.

Kramer cut the engine and coasted in the last fifty yards, getting out and closing his door with care so as not to attract attention. Then he kept close to the hedge and walked up to the garage. It was empty.

"Good morning, my boss," said a voice right behind him.

Turning, he saw one of the Bantu constables there, nervously thumbing the switch on his torch.

"Name?"

"Mkize."

"Well, where's Sergeant Zondi, Mkize?"

"Gone."

"What?"

"Gone away, my boss, I think to the reserves."

"How? My car's still outside there."

"I—I don't know properly, my boss."

"But on whose orders, man? You Kaffirs just can't do what you like, you know! Who said he could go?"

"Actually, I *told* him to go, Lieutenant Kramer," said a side of pork appearing in the doorway.

"Who the—" Kramer just stopped himself.

"Go, boy," the stranger sighed to the Bantu constable, waiting until he had hurried off.

"You were saying?"

This was pork with menaces, no doubt of it.

"I want to know who the hell you are and what the hell you think you're doing."

"No need to get so mad, man. I'm Lieutenant Scott."

"Oh, yes?"

"And I'm just obeying orders."

That last phrase snapped the stem of Kramer's most florid expletive. He stood speechless, staring at the other officer, noting that he was pink and fatty and unclean under the arms. It was amazing how accurate an assessment he had made in that first split second in the half dark. It was equally amazing how determined his mind was to fight shy of assessing just what was going on.

"I've got some coffee in the house. What do you say to us two getting together there and sorting this thing out?"

Kramer made no reply but led the way back into the bungalow through the front door. The coffee was on the desk in the study, a big pot of it and two mugs.

"With milk?"

"Without."

Scott lifted the heavy pot and poured without a tremor. This made Kramer realize he had better ease off on the tension or find himself at a disadvantage.

"Scott, you say? CID?"

"That's right, but not in this division. Been seconded from Southwest for a couple of months."

No wonder Kramer had never heard of the bastard. The Southwest was about as far as you could get from Trekkersburg and still be in the Republic.

"Too much desert?"

"Too much bloody everything out there. Real reason's I needed some experience in towns."

"Still, thought somebody might have told me."

"Only just arrived this morning. Usual bugger-up; nobody knew I was coming, not even your colonel."

"Muller?"

"Du Plessis."

"So he was already in charge when you got here?"

"What do you mean—er—"

"Tromp. Tromp Kramer. Yours?"

"John."

On first-name terms already; not bad going, considering the way Kramer felt. Now to get at the guts of the matter.

"First night and they set you to work, John? You must be a bit pissed off."

"Don't mind. Don't know anyone; barracks aren't up to much. Mind you, I'll find myself a cheap place in a hotel soon as I'm able."

"Uhuh."

"No, the way it happened was this, see? The Colonel called me up to his office around eleven and said that he had a senior officer with his hands full. White bloke murdered and another dead in a car crash, suspicious circumstances."

"Didn't know he cared."

"Oh, yes. Said it was Christmas and he didn't want you too tied up. Also said this murder here seemed pretty straightforward and your boy could probably handle it on his own, seeing it's a Bantu matter."

"Isn't that presuming a bit much?"

"Well, isn't it Bantu?"

Kramer shrugged.

"And your boy is not bad, the Colonel tells me."

"True."

"There you are then. Simple."

Yes, it was simple. Straightforward, like the man said. Nothing to get all worked up about. Yet . . .

"I see, John. So you've taken over from me, in other words. Pity nobody—"

"They couldn't get hold of you."

"No? So what are your plans?"

"None. I've had the kitchen cleaned up, I've seen that Swart's fiancée has been informed—did it by phone, got the Cape Town boys to go round. Lucky she was on night duty."

"And what else?"

"Nothing else. Zondi seems to know what he's doing. Got the home address of the servant and pushed off to find him."

"On foot? How far is it?"

Scott laughed, motioning Kramer to be seated, too.

"Hell, no. He lives in northern Natal, Robert's Halt. I was told to hand over the car they gave me and keep the other for you."

Kramer sat down and put his feet back on the blotter. Actually, once you got over his appearance, and natural distrust of an Afrikaner with an English name, this Scott bloke seemed all right. Not so much pork as pawn, he decided.

"Family?" asked Scott.

"Me? No, why?"

"Christmas Day tomorrow. Just wondered what you'd be doing."

"Nothing special. Got this accident case, of course, but nobody's going to be much help until the twenty-seventh."

"I know. Local lab have already told me they don't want to know about this one till then. I could send the stuff down to Durban, I suppose. Maybe we could have a few drinks?"

"Maybe," Kramer replied, looking very hard at the blotter to the right of his shoes. He was certain that something had been lying there earlier that had since disappeared. Then he glanced up at the bookshelves; they had seemed very neat and orderly before, and he knew Van der Poel had not touched any of the volumes. Casually he pulled open the bottom left drawer and saw a paper clip lying on a Catholic Truth Society pamphlet.

"You've been digging around in this room?" he asked Scott.

"Thought you'd done the job for me, Tromp."

"Ah, so they told you. Just didn't want you to have extra work."

"Thanks, man. You're going now?"

"Just for a pee," Kramer replied, clowning a stiff-legged walk for a couple of paces.

In the bathroom along the passage he opened the medicine cabinet and found what he wanted. He used the lavatory, dallied a moment at the kitchen door, and then rejoined Scott.

"Somebody made a good job of cleaning up in there," he said affably. "Best when they bleed on lino; carpet has to be chucked away. Who did it?"

"Local station sent a boy over."

So the Bantu constables had not left their posts. He would have to take the matter further.

"Think I'll get a bit of shut-eye, John."

"Here?"

"Good as any this time of day. How about you?"

"Seems a good idea. Okay."

"Get a boy to wake me at six when they change over, all right?"

"Fine, Tromp. Me, I'll find myself a proper bed."

Scott left Kramer alone and very soon he was, contrary to his expectations, sound asleep.

Several times a check was made on this.

At ten past six, without seeing Scott again, Kramer took his leave of 44 Sunderland Avenue and drove, not back into town, but toward Skaapvlei police station. In under a mile he sighted his quarry and cut him off.

The Bantu constable reared his bicycle up over the curb, wobbled wildly, caught his balance, and stopped. He was a very startled man. And that made a good beginning.

Kramer swung open his passenger door and called, "Get in—I have something for you."

The constable got in, seating himself on the extreme off side of the car, like a virgin at a drive-in.

"This," said Kramer, holding out a pill. "You swallow that for me."

Which put the constable in a dilemma, but Kramer's rank, skin, and expression reduced his degree of choice. He gulped the aspirin down, swallowing hard because his mouth must have gone very dry.

"It is medicine, my boss?"

"No, it is magic."

33

"*Yebobo!*"

"A special magic that will kill your seed."

The constable, shocked to the core, jabbered in Zulu and Kramer recognized the word for "sterile," which he had been trying to remember.

"That's right, you've got the picture. Only this can't happen if you tell me the truth, old son."

"My—my boss?"

"Tell me the truth and never tell anyone I spoke with you."

The constable nodded. Anything, anything to preserve the family line.

"Then who has been in that house tonight since I left it? Zondi?"

"No, he never go inside. He go away like I say before."

"The other lieutenant?"

"Just him, my boss. No other new ones came."

"Sure?"

"Mkize tells truth, cross my heart."

"The back door was locked, wasn't it?"

"No key for it."

"Right. Off you go then; you did your job well."

The Bantu constable scrambled out and regained the safety of the sidewalk.

"Oh, one other thing, Mkize—may they never fall off."

With which Kramer accelerated away and made for home. It had been a dirty trick to play on the wog, but by going for the Zulu's most vulnerable spot he had made sure of the truth.

When he had left the house with Strydom, everyone—Fingerprints, photographers, the lot—had already been and gone. Zondi had not gone back in. This meant that Scott had been lying in his teeth when he denied making a search in the study.

What this, in turn, actually signified was now the important thing. Kramer thought very carefully and long, finally coming up with what had to be the answer: the bastards really were out to get him, and Zondi, too.

Colonel Du Plessis had separated them by picking on the only other

34

death going to preoccupy Kramer, and then cleverly substituting an officer of equal rank in his place. The fact that praise had been poured on Zondi indicated the devilment of their plans. Plans that had two objectives, and either way they had to win. Plan A was to cause aggravation by splitting the team, hoping the wog, left so much on his own, would mess things up. Plan B was to have Scott see if he could not find another solution to the killing—one which Kramer and Zondi had not supposed existed.

He could just picture the scene when Colonel Muller returned and was handed the Swart report.

Plan A: After all, they would say, if Kramer was willing to have Zondi do so much of the investigating, so were we—the lieutenant is highly respected. We saw no reason to alter the arrangements, although now we know our confidence was unfounded.

Plan B: Well, it seems Zondi decided it was the Bantu domestic, sir —maybe that's why Lieutenant Kramer slipped up in the house. It was just as well Lieutenant Scott took over when he did, or we'd never have found out. Of course you must be disappointed, Colonel Muller, but some of us have been wondering about those two. You know what we mean?

Either way they had to win—providing, however, something *did* go wrong. For the first time in years, Kramer found himself carefully appraising Zondi's capabilities, testing—with complete honesty—how much confidence he had in the man; after all, both their careers depended upon it. But Zondi was not found wanting, and Kramer felt sure he would make it to Robert's Halt and do the necessary without any trouble. Which shifted the onus to himself. Granted his examination of the house had not been exhaustive, yet the case hardly demanded it should be: open and shut, was the expression he wanted. Granted he might have gone over the study more carefully; but Scott had done so, and was still loafing about, and this indicated nothing had come up. No, the likelihood of Plan B ever bearing fruit was very slight.

So back to Plan A and a counterplan. If Zondi was going to come unstuck because his boss was not around, then the absurd reason for his absence could, with a little help, be made twice as absurd. And absurdity was something that got Colonel Muller's goat but good.

"I shall go to absurd, but absurd, lengths," vowed Kramer aloud to himself, finding a café at which to have breakfast. "*Ach*, man, but the mind will bloody boggle!"

His mind would, ultimately.

four

Breakfast comprised an entire packet of streaky bacon, a loaf of fresh white bread, and a family-size bottle of strawberry pop, consumed with gusto at the side of the national road north. Zondi was uncertain what his day would bring, and anxious to ensure missed meals would not trouble him. He would have lit a fire for the meat, but farmers could be trigger happy at this time of year.

To be sure, the grass was very dry, and one ember could easily have the low hills of grazing swept black in minutes. A bleak, blond land, with scattered thornbush making smudges of dull green like white women's eyeshadow, and bare patches of earth the pinky red of their sunburn. A hard land, too, that gave nothing for nothing. A good place for puff adders and lizards and the shrikes that hung their prey on the barbed-wire fences.

His watch had stopped and the car had no radio. But judging by the sun, it was still before eight. Plenty of time to smoke a Stuyvesant and take another look at the map. At least the car, a beaten-up Anglia, had this much that was useful in it.

Zondi had about another ten kilometers to do on the tar, then he turned right and carried on along a district road—its number was illegible. Five kilometers of this, then a turning left past a mission. Then, only two kilometers beyond that, the trading store and small hamlet of Robert's Halt.

He was thankful not to be in a hurry once the corrugations of the dirt road, regular as those in a washboard, began to drum beneath four very doubtful tires. There were also potholes big enough to swallow a wheel and sharp stones that clattered like hail on the car's underside. The dust, however, was the worst of the lot, making short work of the ill-fitting doors and covering everything. But he was glad to be in a car and not, as long ago, on the seat of a donkey cart beside his father. Then the stones had been the worst as passing vehicles shotgunned them up at you. Once he had been hit on the ear—which was better luck than the donkey had met with on another occasion, when it lost an eye.

Through a line of gums and wattles on the left appeared several whitewashed concrete-block buildings dominated by a tin-roofed church. From the size of the cross above it, Zondi guessed Roman Catholic and then saw a sign that read: "St. Bernard's Mission School and Hospital." It seemed strangely deserted for a school, although the pupils could still be in assembly. Which did not, however, account for the fact that no patients were visible, and that was odd. Still, none of this was any of his business—that lay not a kilometer away over the ridge.

The Anglia churned its way up, spending a nasty ten seconds with its inside wheels deep in a rut, then topped the rise and slithered to a halt. In the valley below was Robert's Halt, hidden in among more gums and wattles. This happened to suit Zondi's purpose perfectly, for he had decided that a slow, deceptively casual stroll up to Shabalala's side would be preferable to a hard sprint after him.

He took the car off the road and locked it. Then he pulled his old trick of turning his jacket inside out—which was what most rustics did, being very taken with the shiny satin lining—and checked his shoulder holster for snags. All set.

It was a good day for walking, not nearly as hot as the previous one, and the air in the valley very clear. Zondi first watched swifts swallowing insects in the sky, then looked to see what quality of cattle grazed the slopes around. He saw none. He listened for the zipping whistles of the herd boys keeping their charges together on dipping day, but heard none.

He stopped. This place was indeed very peculiar. If an ache in his body had not persisted to remind him of how he had spent the night, he would have cursed himself for drinking too much. Even so, had he sunk an oil drum of Moses Makatini's moonshine, Robert's Halt would still have seemed unreal.

There was nothing tangible he could deduce from his observations, but they bred caution within him. So he found a cross-country route to the trading store which would allow him to approach unnoticed—the path was so overgrown he had little chance of meeting anyone else on it, either.

As he descended toward the river, Zondi began to hear sounds as confusing as everything else: dull thuds and scraping and the squeal of metal, yet no voices. By then he should have been close enough to hear even a child laugh.

The branches thinned and he saw Robert's Halt across the river—and a sight quite extraordinary. The place was surrounded by policemen, the whites armed with sten guns and the Africans with spears. Their riot vans unfortunately blocked off a proper view of what was going on beyond them.

Zondi cursed. Cursed and swore because he had been given a car without a radio. There must have been sudden, dramatic developments in the case he was unaware of.

As he continued walking toward the hamlet, his mind struggled with conjecture, tried to think of what possible reason there could be for such a turnout. Even if Shabalala had taken a gun from Swart's home, and was expected to resist arrest, six men at the most would have been sufficient for the job.

The thuds and squeals ceased.

Zondi checked his step, slipping behind an aloe to see what happened next. There was the sound of an engine starting up and then, from behind the riot vans, came a truck piled high with villagers and their property.

What an idiot he had been: it was an eviction. An ordinary Black Spot eviction, one of hundreds, an everyday event—and he had allowed his imagination to distort his vision. Of course there were thuds when furniture was loaded on a truck; naturally there were noises when valuable roof sheeting was stripped off to be removed as well; obviously it was not a time for talk, nor for children to laugh. As for the cordon of police, that was standard procedure to prevent any stupidity.

A bulldozer roared into raucous life and emerged from the scrub to flatten the vacated homes. It waited, however, for three other trucks to carry away the last of the people. They forded the river close to where Zondi stood and he could see no men among them, except for the very old. Certainly nobody resembling the description he had been given of Shabalala.

Which was hardly surprising. With the Force out in force, Robert's Halt was the last place a killer on the run would want to be that particular morning.

The Trekkersburg police mortuary was a squat red-brick structure almost undetectable in a dip in the long grass and weeds behind the barracks. From the low viewpoint afforded the driver of a modern American car, it was, in fact, invisible; you just had to commit yourself to a well-worn, twisting track that revealed all rather suddenly.

Kramer braked hard and drew his Chevrolet in beside the Pontiac owned by Strydom. Only one window in the four deadpan walls was at eye level; through it he could see Sergeant Van Rensburg in the office taking a fortifying nip of Cape brandy. Van Rensburg fortunately did not see him; the man was a tiresome bastard at the best of times.

First the fly screen and then the big metal doors, a sudden chill that was not entirely a matter of temperature, and the familiar sight of Strydom up to his elbows in another man. Enjoying every moment of it, too.

"Aha!" said Strydom, bringing out a brace of lungs and taking them over to the sluice.

"Sis," said Kramer, lighting up.

Strydom let the water run, then sliced open the spongy organs, scraping at their interior with his scalpel.

"Well, where's our friend then, doc?"

"Third table along."

"*That* thing?"

"I hinted as much last night, Lieutenant. Proper human concertina. Propped the top over there so it wouldn't roll off."

Van Rensburg had been busy with his water spray and—it seemed—with a comb. For Mark Clive Wallace, white male aged forty, had both a clean face and a part as he stared across at Kramer from a shallow bowl on the instrument cabinet. He looked a friendly sort.

"Hello, old mate," said Kramer, stooping to look Wallace in the eye that was open. "Tell me, what did you get up to?"

"One hell of a lot of booze in his belly, for a start, Lieutenant. Not so much in his blood, though. Must've belted down a few very fast just before it happened."

"I'll find something to fit that then. What else?"

"I'd swear his hands weren't on the wheel when he hit the guard rail. You see, you'd normally expect at least fractures of the thumbs, here at the base. My guess is that he had them over his peepers."

"What'd make him do that?"

"A bright light?"

"Not bad, doc. Or maybe he just didn't want to see where he was going."

"Suicide?"

"A theory."

"The only other thing I can tell you is that he hadn't eaten since breakfast."

"How was his health?"

"Not bad at all. Nothing terminal—and no ulcer either, if that's what you're thinking."

Kramer continued his examination of the three-dimensional mug shot, noting the parenthesis of smile lines bracketing the wide mouth, and the ebullience of the upswept mustache. It was not the face of a man who lightly took his own life.

"Could be he just misjudged and panicked, doc," he murmured.

"I'll go along with you on that."

"But still that fool Du Plessis—"

Strydom would doubtless have been sympathetic had not Van Rensburg entered at that moment with a clipboard ready to take notes.

"Morning, Lieutenant! Another scorcher of a day, hey?"

Van Rensburg tipped his head, listening, and Kramer noticed the tin roof had begun to plink as it expanded under a fierce sun. He wondered what the weather was like upcountry, wherever it was Zondi had gone. And he hoped to God all was going according to plan.

Zondi had sat for a long while in the spiked shade of the aloe, watching the police party ensure the total destruction of Robert's Halt. He watched them dispatch abandoned dogs and then sit down to a picnic tea. He watched the horseplay that followed. He watched a dung beetle carve a perfect sphere from a pile of droppings near his feet.

Finally he decided there was nothing to be gained from going across, identifying himself, and asking about Shabalala. Nobody would know anything: personal details were never the concern of eviction squads. He also encountered problems when asking favors of officers unknown to him. Besides, they were unlikely to believe his story of having been sent out alone to catch a white man's murderer.

But the basic reason behind his reluctance to involve others rested on the fact that being allowed the initiative was a true compliment—one he intended repaying with a nice neck for the gallows.

There were now signs that the squad would soon be returning to base. The officer in charge kept looking around to the west, where, above the wooded escarpment, cloud was massing with astonishing swiftness, piling up like shaving cream from the lieutenant's aerosol can. In another hour, sky drums would beat and long legs of lightning begin their dance, stamping death into the dust. Nobody who had a choice wanted to be around for that.

And this included Zondi, who also then realized that the sight of the Anglia beside the road might bring complications. So, with a final glance at what had once been a simple solution, he began back up the hill through the thorn scrub; trying to assess, as he sprinted, the best way of getting a lead on Shabalala's present whereabouts. A rain bird accompanied him part of the way, heralding the all too obvious. Then it flew on in the direction of the mission and proved itself a real help.

"Mission!" Zondi grunted, unlocking both the car and his tardy thought processes. There someone was bound to have information about the Shabalala family which could be useful.

He reached the mission gate within minutes and clanked in over the cattle grid. The place appeared deserted, apart from a few hens near the borehole, and only the rising wind murmured as he parked around the back, out of sight of the road. The feeling this gave him was not good.

Then, as he sat there, opening a fresh pack of Stuyvesant, Zondi discerned a second murmuring, as solemn as the sound made by the press of air through the trees, but rising and falling in a repetitious rhythm. It was a human sound—it was prayer.

He replaced the king-size, made certain his shoulder-holster straps were hidden, and got out of the car. The scent of eucalyptus from the blue gums was evocative, taking him back many years to his own mission school in a remote valley of Zululand. There the best dreams of his life had been dreamed; all you had to do, the white nuns had said, was learn your lessons well and then, when you grew up, you could be anything you wanted to be. They had been wrong, those stupid, kind women, who believed all men were brothers, totally wrong, but Zondi still could not feel bitter. Unlike his classmate Matthew Mslope, who had gone back with a mob to burn, pillage, and rape. But Matthew had been wrong, too, and Zondi had arrested him, had him hanged. Which was how he met the lieutenant. And how two wrongs could make a right, whatever Sister Therese had said.

Smiling, Zondi started toward the church, not quite certain he could remember the rosary but willing to give it a try. He pushed open the door to the wattle-and-daub building and saw, after adjusting to the dim light within, that seven nuns and a white lay brother were kneeling at the far communion rail. Only the man turned at the sound of the intrusion, yet looked away again almost immediately, his expression unchanged. Zondi tiptoed down the aisle, then knelt behind a pew made from a plank laid across two old oil drums.

"Hail Mary, full of grace . . ." The words were there without his thinking, strangely comforting, like Miriam's brown breasts beneath his cheek when, afterward, they slept, the hard day done. "Pray for us now, and at the hour of our death. Amen."

Nevertheless, Zondi sensed a tension, one that had been there even before his presence was noted. It kept his body stiff and his mind racing. But the possible reason for it evaded him.

Another decade of the rosary began and, in the thatch overhead, some small creature, probably a mouse, dislodged a straw, which wafted down in a slow spiral. Before it reached the earth floor there was the sound of a Land-Rover lurching up outside. Zondi rose.

So did the lay brother, who, with a quick gesture, bade him enter the crude confessional, which had been nailed together out of powdered-milk crates and curtained by a well-wisher's cast-off brocade. The idea was a good one—and he took advantage of it immediately. Through one of the many gaps in its side he kept an eye on the door.

Half a minute later the officer in charge of the eviction squad entered the church, swaggering in with a swagger stick, which he slapped for emphasis on the palm of his left hand.

"Hey, you," he said, addressing the religious, still at their prayers. "Where's the priest?"

The lay brother advanced toward him, stopping two yards short.

"Father Lofthouse went with the people yesterday. I'm Brother Kerrigan."

"Why's he not back yet?"

"I cannot say. Perhaps there was a lot he had to do."

"The government looks after the people."

"Of course, but he has his spiritual duties."

"Like hell. A troublemaker, that's what he is."

"I don't think so."

"And you? What are you doing here alone with all these black women?"

"Nothing."

"Oh, really?"

"We were praying together."

"For your dearly departed, hey?"

44

The officer, six of whom could pull an ox wagon, enjoyed his little joke —if nobody else did. However, it had the effect of mellowing him somewhat and he put his stick away, poking it down his right stocking. Then he dusted his hands together.

"Whole bang-shoot's gone," he said with satisfaction. "By tonight they'll all be resettled in the homelands."

"Homelands?" echoed the lay brother, his tone ironic.

"Man, sometimes I think it's a shame I can't send *you* lot back to *your* homelands," the officer replied with a grin.

"I may be a Kerrigan, officer, but do I speak with an Irish accent?" The grin turned lean.

"What's that got to do with it?"

Very little, conceded Brother Kerrigan with a weary shrug: the term "homelands" being historical rather than factual.

"*Ach*, don't let's argue politics," the officer said, adaptable in his attitudes. "We aren't politicians, are we, hey? Just two blokes that have got to see laws are kept. You've got your Ten Commandments—and I've got my orders from above, hey? Ha ha. There was no trouble."

Brother Kerrigan showed his relief at hearing this. "We told them there would be no point," he said.

"True, man, quite true."

"And?"

"*Ach*, nothing else. Just a social call, you might say."

"I see."

"Best be getting along then. Bye for now."

"God bless," said Brother Kerrigan.

He waited until the cattle grid confirmed the departure of the Land-Rover before rapping on the confessional wall. Zondi emerged, exchanged nods with the nuns, and greeted him formally in Zulu.

"My name is Matthew Mslope," he said.

"Well, Matthew, there's been enough chatter in this church for one morning. You can explain what you're doing here across at the house."

Zondi only just remembered to genuflect before they left the building. His mind was on that explanation.

People had no right to play the arse with their lives just before Christmas, Kramer complained. The festive season was bad enough without any encouragement. But there was nobody in the lift to hear this.

He had paid a call on the new widow, Mrs. Paula Wallace, finding her mindlessly putting up decorations and dabbing her eyes with the cotton wool used to represent snow. Although they had no children, it was what Mark would have wanted, she said. A neighbor was trying to persuade her otherwise, so it was difficult to get a word in. Finally Kramer left, armed with as few facts as a lynch mob.

Which, when boiled down, brought him to where he was at that moment: the fifth floor of the Sanlam Building in the city center. The lift door slid aside to reveal the glass-fronted offices of Montreal Life, a Canadian-based insurance company. Kramer stepped out and paused behind a hedge of gold lettering to weigh up the receptionist.

He put her at one hundred and ten pounds, age nineteen or twenty, and mother tongue indisputably English.

"Lieutenant Kramer," he announced, allowing the spring-loaded door to bang shut behind him. "This the place Mr. Wallace used to work?"

"Who?"

"Mr. Wallace. Was he a nice man?"

"Yes—very."

"Gave you things, did he? Flowers? Chocs? Patted your bum?"

"Pardon?"

"You've got to move faster than that, popsy; caught you there. Anyway, what if he did?"

"What?"

"You heard. You're a good-looker; so what?"

"He . . ."

"Was married?"

"Yer—yes."

"Aren't we all?"

That put things in a new light for her and she pondered a moment before recovery.

"Just you look here," she said, very haughty.

46

"Anytime—it's a pleasure."

"Really! Do you want to see Mr. Cooper, *sir?*"

"Who's he when he's at home?"

"The manager."

"Can sit and twiddle his thumbs for all I care."

"Then who?"

"You, popsy. You're the one I want to talk to."

Kramer was coarse fishing, using a thin line of patter and hoping she would take the bait before noticing the hook. So far, she was interested.

"Oh, I see. I suppose this is your way of —"

"Inviting you to lunch? Right first time."

"Then you can ruddy well take a jump at yourself, whoever you are!"

"Lieutenant Kramer of the Murder Squad, actually. Didn't I say before?"

No, he had not said quite that before—and she noticed.

"Murder?"

A definite nibble.

"Like a little drink first?" Kramer offered, flipping back the counter flap. She got up from the switchboard.

"I— What about Mr. Cooper?"

"Ach, tell him you've got period pains or something."

"Honestly!"

"Meantime," said Kramer, backing away, "I'll go and see a man about a dragon."

Which left her grinning foolishly from ear to pretty ear. Funny; he could always tell the ones who reacted like poodles to their first sniff of a mongrel.

In the Gents near the lift, Kramer dipped his face in a basin of cold water and then held his wrists under the tap. Much refreshed, he patted himself half dry on the roller towel before bending low to check on his hair, the mirror having been positioned by some bastard of a midget getting his own back.

"Saint George, I presume?"

A big man, almost as big as himself, was beaming at Kramer from the doorway over a spotted bow tie and quite a lot else. He glared back.

"Couldn't help overhearing, Montreal Life, my door open, a proper hoot, just had to say hello."

"Mr. Cooper?"

"Christ, no. McDonald."

"Well, Mr. McDonald—"

"Old McDonald. What I usually answer to, as it happens, not that I've ever owned a bloody farm, God knows. Still, who am I to argue with my friends?"

"Mark Wallace was a friend?"

"Friend? Far more than that! Old pals, buddies, taught me all I know, a wonderful person. Proper man's man is Marky boy."

"Was."

"So you say he's dead, too?"

"Of course."

"Jesus, but all this just doesn't seem *real!*" McDonald protested, it seemed in anger. "Hasn't happened at all. Mark dead and a card from him this morning? Impossible."

Kramer watched a bent king-size fumbled into the mouth, and noted how it exaggerated a tremble to measurable proportions. McDonald was in very poor shape. Kramer wondered why.

"How come it's unreal for you?"

"Told you; taught me all I know. Times I've sat with him and talked about his death—"

"Hey?"

"Life, whole life—Christ, the irony!—practicing putting it across, you understand, and Mark saying, 'Come on, son, now it's my turn to die, *mine*—and make me *see* that widow!' "

McDonald choked up.

"How well was he insured?" Kramer asked after a time.

"To the hilt," replied McDonald, with a crooked, crooked smile. "Paula will never want for anything, that's for sure."

"Maybe we can have a chat later?"

"Why not now?"

"I've got myself a date."

"You weren't serious about taking Pat out? You know, Miss Weston, the receptionist?"

"Naturally."

"Please . . ."

"Please what? Please don't?"

McDonald aborted a nod, and gave Kramer an agonized look.

"Don't worry, Mr. McDonald. If she lets on to anything between you and her, I won't be selling it to anyone."

"But you're quite wrong!"

Be that as it may, Kramer suddenly wondered if this was not perhaps a proper case after all. What a triumph that would be.

five

Brother Kerrigan and the seven nuns shared their simple fare with Zondi, and swallowed his story whole. The erasure of Robert's Halt was for them such a momentous event that they missed the fact that its actual news value hardly warranted a first-hand report.

"Excellent, excellent," applauded Brother Kerrigan. "The more people who know about this, the better. Did you take any photos, Matthew?"

"Some snaps, but I have not got a lens that can reach a long way."

"Then go back this afternoon, now they've gone."

"My editor thinks it is more important that I do a write-up on the resettlement area."

"The dumping ground? Isn't that a bit risky?"

Zondi, in his role as the case-hardened chief reporter for a Zulu weekly, shrugged modestly.

"Maybe you can lend me the collar of a priest; the government does not stop you going in."

The nuns giggled appreciatively, even the greedy one whose mouth was full, and passed the beaker of soured milk down to their guest. Then they pressed on him another sardine. It astonished Zondi that they were all so recklessly trusting—he had not offered any proof of his assumed identity. But then they were probably accustomed to sympathetic strangers who, out of deference to their own position, revealed very little about themselves. Both sides of the coin had their virtues.

"You say, Holy Brother, that these people today were not everybody from Robert's Halt?"

"Just Brother will do, Matthew. . . . No, they weren't. Half went yesterday."

"Like thirty?"

"Forty-five, to be precise. Look for yourself; I've the Father's list here."

Brother Kerrigan reached around for a school tablet and gave it to Zondi, who looked down the column of names and found *Shabalala* in the middle. The word seemed to rise in relief.

"How long was it that the government gave the people to make ready?"

One of the nuns tut-tutted and the others sighed.

"Well, naturally there's been talk about this Black Spot for some time. Father Lofthouse did what he could. Went round to the farmers, wrote letters, saw them at BAD. Even petitioned the Archbishop. But nothing could be done."

Brother Kerrigan, true to his calling, swiveled again in his chair to produce the appropriate textual references—a bulky bundle of exchanges with the department of Bantu Administration and Development. Zondi hardly glanced at them.

"But how long, Brother?"

"It happened out of the blue, finally. An official from BAD came by three days ago, told the people the talking was over, and the police and lorries arrived yesterday morning."

Time factors are always of vital importance in detective work—only Zondi did not much care for the simple explanation that now suggested itself. He forced it aside. He stood up.

"Many thanks," he said, "but it is time that I go on to this place. It is the one near Blitzkop, is that not so?"

"Heavens, no, Matthew. Much further on. Called Jabula, believe it or not."

"Kilometers, please?"

"At least a hundred and fifty."

"*Hau!* This I was not told! What is the time?"

"Two. But you'll still go, I hope?"

Zondi wound his watch.

"Maybe. First I must speak with my boss on the telephone."

"You could do that from here."

Zondi gave him a look as old-fashioned as the walnut instrument with its crank handle in the corner, and everyone laughed nervously. It was a widespread belief that private telephones, even on mission stations, had long since lost their innocence.

"Then we won't keep you—you'd have had to go back to the main road anyway to reach Jabula. There's a whites-only kiosk at the first service station, but the old chap there isn't too fussy; he's a Pole."

Zondi took his leave of the nuns on the veranda and, avoiding the storm puddles, walked in silence with Brother Kerrigan to the car. It balked like a mule but finally got going.

"Difficult times, Matthew," said Brother Kerrigan, stepping away from the driver's window with a wave.

Zondi waved back, but was through the gate before replying, "Too damn right, boss!"

And then he drove very close to the limit along the dangerously muddy road, skidding and drifting, and not caring very much if he came unstuck. It was as though he was tempting fate into providing him with an honorable way out of the mess he had made; not that he had oblivion in mind, rather a few days' blissful concussion and some sick leave.

It was totally unlike him to think like this, but then it was equally unlike him to jump so quickly to conclusions. He tried to work out what had made him feel so confident that Shabalala presented a sitting target, and found some of the blame could be shared with the lieutenant, whose mood the night before had been altogether very strange. But no, that was not just: the lieutenant had not prevented him from making checks at the bus and railway stations, nor had he dissuaded him from alerting informers in the townships. He, Zondi, had himself decided on the dawn departure for Robert's Halt. Because he, Zondi, could not wait to show them what a clever Kaffir he was. *Slima!*

This obscenity doubled its work load as Zondi diverted his anger to a blue Volkswagen that unexpectedly overtook him, shouldering the Anglia almost into the ditch. It was out of sight in seconds, but he got its number: NTK 4544. For the next kilometer or so, he drove on at a more moderate speed, preoccupied by wondering what a Trekkersburg vehicle was doing so far from home, and then by the puzzle of where it had come from in the immediate sense—he was still on the section that ended at Robert's Halt. Then he recalled seeing a farm signposted and dropped the matter.

When his thoughts returned to the Shabalala affair, his mind was much calmer and prepared to negotiate. First of all, the nature of the mess had to be established: very simply, Shabalala was not where he had been expected to be, Zondi had no idea of where to look next, and time was being wasted with both his own and the lieutenant's reputation at stake. Calling in help was out of the question. So that meant he had to somehow narrow down the search again to a specific, limited area. And the best way of doing this was by acting on information received—but from whom? The town wife, Lucy, perhaps, and maybe other servants in Sunderland Avenue. The bus-ticket clerk or the orange seller in Trichaard Street. All were potential sources of fresh leads, but all were a very long way away and it would take hours to reach them.

It would not take as long, he suddenly realized, as he turned onto the national road, to do as he had promised the missionaries and go to Jabula. If anyone was able to supply a list of relatives and other possible harborers of the fugitive, it was his family. Never mind whether they wanted to impart this information; he would get it. Oh, yes, and quickly, too.

Kramer rang in from a call box in the vestibule of the Bayswater Hotel, keeping one eye on Pat Weston at her table on the veranda. They had not as yet got down to business and she could not be left alone for too long.

"Hello, Lieutenant Scott? John? Tromp Kramer here."

"How's it, man?"

"Just giving you a bell about those drinks we were going to have. Is it still on, hey?"

"Okay by me. When?"

"Around five. Saloon bar at the Albert Hotel."

"See you then, Tromp."

"Hey, just a sec—how's the case going?"

"You mean your bloke Zondi?"

Kramer tried to keep the deep breath he took to himself.

"Shabalala. Any news?"

"Only there's no such place as Robert's Halt."

"Since when? Christ, I've been—"

"Since yesterday, Tromp."

"*Hey?*"

"Black Spot removal. Saw it ten minutes ago on the daily report from up near there."

This time Kramer just let his breath hiss out and the hell with it.

"So it seems your boy is having all the luck," Scott said. "Man, it's a problem. Colonel Du Plessis wants me to go up there myself, maybe organize a manhunt in the hills. What do you think? You know this Zondi—can he cope?"

"*Ach*, he'll cope."

"Sure? Colonel Dupe—"

"I'm certain, man, John. Anyway, I thought we'd fixed for some drinks. You want to go arsing about in the veld on Christmas Eve? Must be bloody mad. There's no relatives in this case to worry about. If I were you, I'd give Zondi till the day after Boxing Day to come up with something—nobody'll be interested before then. And you can't tell me that Du Plessis is going to miss his pudding for this one either."

Scott laughed. "Maybe you're right, Tromp."

"Right? Course I'm right!"

"See you at five then."

The receiver at the other end went down, leaving the one in Kramer's hand bleeping *wrong wrong wrong*. He should have given himself time to think. In his hurry to protect Zondi's interests, he had forgotten his own. Now, should the investigation fail to deliver within two days, Scott could quite justifiably pass him the buck. And with the kind of odds Zondi was facing out there, the chances of that happening were very great. So great the Colonel was probably in for his best Christmas goody in years: Kramer and Zondi, the pair of them, in one fell swoop.

An Indian waiter knocked hesitantly on the glass and pointed out a hotel guest who wanted to make a call. Kramer replaced the receiver, took his drink, and left the booth.

Wrong. There was a lot that was wrong with the Shabalala case, when you paused to consider. It was wrong that he had been taken off it, and it was wrong that Scott had not done anything himself all day—at least, that was how it seemed. It was also wrong that Colonel Du Plessis had not simply ordered that manhunt without consulting Scott first, and probably even wrong that it had not been tackled on a large scale right from the start. But most troubling was the *wrong feeling* Kramer had experienced on his return to Sunderland Avenue, when he had noticed little changes in the study, and thought something was missing. Behind it all was an elusive . . .

"I thought you'd never be coming," said Miss Weston, putting away her powder compact.

Oh, God, you never got a proper chance to think.

"Sorry, Pat. Duty before pleasure, hey?"

"It's getting late. I wanted to do some last-minute shopping."

"Gone off me, have you?"

"What gives you the idea I was ever on?"

"When I went to the bog you undid your two top buttons, am I right?"

She blushed pink as a carbon monoxide stiff and covered her cleavage with a spread hand. Then she tried to push her chair back but the cane legs caught in the coconut matting.

"You Afrikaans," she said. "You're as crude as my father's always said. I'm used to gentlemen!"

"Afrikaans is a language, Miss Weston," Kramer replied, smiling pleasantly, with an effort. "I am an *Afrikaner*. But talking of gentlemen, which one in particular? Mr. Mark Wallace, Esquire?"

"I'm going!"

"But you won't!"

"Huh! So you think!"

Kramer made no move to restrain her, but leaned back and stretched.

"Why not?" she snapped.

"Because you don't want to miss the rest of the show."

She was half out of her seat when she stopped to stare quizzically at him. Slowly a wry smile appeared and as slowly she sat down again.

"Is that what it is, Lieutenant? I'm fascinated. Tell me, where do you get all your ideas—the bioscope?"

"Nice guess. Walt Disney mostly. *Lady and the Tramp*, y'know."

"I'm flattered!"

"How do you think I feel? Playing up to you as a member of the inferior breed. All sniff and let's get on with it."

"Daddy—"

"*Ach*, of course he has said that, too, Miss Weston! I wasn't bloody born yesterday."

When she blushed this time, she went pink as a schoolgirl. Poor kid.

"I—I'm sorry, Lieutenant."

"No need. My mistake for letting it get personal."

And Kramer meant that. He had pushed it too far. This was just another reminder that ever since his arrival at Swart's house the night before, he had not been quite himself. In trying to make something of the Wallace case, he had been forcing the pace all along. To cap it all, now he had somehow dragged in the Widow Fourie's children and the cartoon treat he had given them at the Durban drive-in. Which was entirely the sort of thinking he wanted most to avoid. Still no word from her.

"You said Murder Squad."

"Hey? Oh, yes. Well, all suspicious deaths fall into this category until we sort them out, you see. And 'suspicious' can also mean just deaths that don't make ordinary sense."

"What's the mystery in a car crash? Every week we've got customers who—"

"Can't reveal anything at this stage."

"Okay. Don't then. Can I finish the sandwiches?"

"Please. Now let's get something out of the way right at the start: How did you get on with Mr. Wallace?"

This time the question was phrased and uttered so gently she did not even glance up, but went on carefully teasing the fat from the ham filling with her fingers.

"To be honest, I thought he was very attractive—most of us girls did at the Montreal. He was always polite and cheerful and he *didn't* pat our bottoms, unlike one I could name."

"Old McDonald?"

She laughed, winking over the neat bite she made in the bread.

"What you said about presents was almost right, Lieutenant, because every birthday—and I've had three there—he's brought in a posy and said his wife made it."

"Uhuh."

"Only I know the stall in the market where they come from! Poor Mr. Wallace."

Kramer changed position, leaning forward and cupping his chin in his hands, assuming the absorbed pose of the gossip-gatherer—a technique he should have thought of in the first place. She brought her chair in a little closer on reflex and then they were all girls together.

"Like that, was it, Pat?"

"Well, it's just guesswork really, but I've been on switchboard long enough to be right pretty often."

"Hard on him?"

"Terrible. Nag, nag, nag. Every time their servants did anything she'd want him back to threaten them with the sack."

"Hell," murmured Kramer, amused by this unwitting confession of eavesdropping.

"Oh, yes. The times I've taken it on myself to give him a warning buzz so he can decide whether he'll talk to her."

"These other girls you spoke about—they found him attractive, too?"

"Not as much as me, I suppose. You see, I thought we had a lot more in common, even if he was a bit square."

"You must be very upset, Pat."

"I am and I'm not. It's a feeling like someone crying deep down inside of me."

But she pushed away the plate with half a round still on it.

"What was I saying?"

"That Mr. Wallace was a bit square. How about triangles?"

His tone was carefully confidential, probing.

"It wouldn't be right."

"Why not?"

"Because I was never quite sure."

"Go on, you can tell me. It can't hurt him now—and it just could help us if there is something, or somebody rather, behind this."

"Well," she said, glad to have been coaxed out of having a bad conscience, "well, I think that Mr. Wallace found himself a girl friend six months ago."

"Uhuh?"

"Little things a man wouldn't notice—but I did. I saw him as he came out of the lift, you see, before he changed back into his usual self."

"You're bright, aren't you? More."

"There isn't any."

"Hey?"

"Anyway, he's been very down in the dumps for two weeks now— was, I mean—so it must have ended."

"And that's all?"

"Yes."

"No theories as to who it was?"

"None. Besides, he didn't really have time."

"Oh, come on."

"He didn't. He arrived at the office at eight, right? Went out for half an hour at eleven to change his library book, stayed in at lunchtime and ate from a tray the office boy fetched from the tearoom, went home at five on the dot. If I had to ring him, he'd be there by five-thirty."

Kramer examined her face carefully, trying to detect in it a deliberate attempt to withhold information—what had started out as a promising sidelight on Mark Wallace had certainly taken a nosedive. But she passed the test.

"Which is why you weren't sure? You couldn't fit your feeling and the timing together?"

"I suppose so. Yes, that's it, and why I didn't really want to say anything."

"Just suppose you were right, though. What would his wife have done?"

"Her? If that bitch had caught him up to something, she'd have—"

"Thanks, Miss Weston."

It was best the girl should rush off to do her shopping without feeling her lunch hour had been wasted. There was no other justification for leading her into that final, contrived remark, cut short as it had been by shocked pseudo-realization.

For Kramer knew damn well that Mrs. Paula Wallace could no sooner rig a fatal car accident than get a fairy to stand upright on her Christmas tree. When he had started on about triangles, he had been looking for a bloke in the other apex, not a phantom floozy. Some ingenious lover boy who wanted husband Mark out of the way. Of course there could always have been another triangle—Wallace, floozy and *her* lawful spouse. . . .

"*Ach,* rubbish," he said, inadvertently attracting the attention of a waiter.

"Suh?"

The point of it all eluded him. He went back to basics. Here was an ordinary accident to which he was giving the full treatment. He wanted to know something about the victim, so he had tried that fine source of office and home truths, the switchboard girl. What she had to say was vague and sentimental and probably half daydreams. Take that nonsense about Wallace changing as he stepped into his work place; it was a tired, sad little trick practiced daily by millions. All that her confidences established was that Wallace had been, in the more acceptable sense of the word, one of her gentlemen. And a dull henpecked hubby to boot. Which was, in all fairness, as much as you could expect out of a freak pileup.

Yet Kramer felt a fret of frustration and the drag of disappointment. Hell, of course! Man, he was slipping. It was McDonald's behavior, his blatant anxiety over Pat Weston, which had set a level of expectation for the interview. It had never been reached.

He paid for his drink and sank it quickly. The logic of it was simple. Number one, as McDonald had claimed, and as Pat Weston had made plain, there was nothing between those two. Number two, this meant McDonald feared she would tell the police something about Wallace which he also knew but would keep to himself. Number three, McDonald had assumed *incorrectly* that Pat Weston was in possession of such information. Number four, all Kramer need do was pretend to McDonald that she had, in fact, spilled some beans, and see what happened next.

As he had done his shopping, there was no time like the present.

Zondi saw the blue Volkswagen again, quite by chance. He had traveled far into an undulating countryside, so eroded and barren it was like taking a close look at the dirt road itself. Any thorn trees had long since disappeared, and so had any grass that was good for cattle—goats were the only livestock capable of survival on the dry spikes that remained. Sure enough, he saw a few of them to begin with, and the huddles of huts from which they had wandered, but then no others beyond a forlorn trading store with a rusted hole in its rain-water tank. This was when the drive had become thoroughly monotonous, and his speed along the seldom-used byway proportionately greater. And so, through accident rather than design, he achieved what few men, however skillfully they strived, ever achieved—he hit a rising guinea fowl full-on with the nose of his car.

It happened just around a tight bend on the shoulder of a hill and the impact was considerable. A loud thud, a splatter of blood, and another thud as it bounced off the roof. He slammed on his brakes and went into a zigzag skid, finishing up a good hundred yards farther on. Cursing at the delay, he jumped out and wiped the windshield, black feathers with white polka dots confirming his split-second diagnosis.

Then he looked back up the road. The guinea fowl must have spun off into the boulders and aloes, for it was nowhere to be seen. A pity, because he would have liked to retrieve such a delectable trophy, but searching for it would take up too much time.

So he drove on again, making the gearbox howl for mercy as he wrenched the most from each ratio before shifting to the next. This occupied him for the best part of a kilometer before he thought of looking at his watch. The truth was he had made very good time. And there was the possibility that a guinea fowl would make a first-class enticement if he had to resort to bartering with Shabalala's neighbors for a tip-off.

Yet another kilometer went by before he made up his mind to turn back. It seemed much farther than it should be, but finally the skid marks showed up on the slope ahead. He left the Anglia well off the road and began looking for the dead bird, anxious now that some passing predator had not beaten him to it. He was crouched low in the rocks, mourning a mangled, quite inedible mess, when he heard the whine of a Volkswagen engine.

And looked up to catch no more than a glimpse of NTK 4544 diving down in the direction of Jabula.

It was a touching sight. Two angels knelt before McDonald's desk and sang loudly of a Silent Night. Their voices were sweet if their diction was terrible. Kramer paused in the doorway, highly amused.

"That's enough. Lovely, happy Christmas," said the embarrassed McDonald, hastily handing them each some change, which was snatched away into the engulfing bed sheets.

Then the angels, whose wings were pinned-on pages of newspaper carefully torn, tried to make their exit.

"Not so fast, you *skelms*," said Kramer, barring the way. "Is that you inside there, Ephraim?"

"*Hau*, Boss Kramer!"

The slightly taller of the two African children pulled back his sheet and grinned up at him.

"Doing good business?"

"*Lambele, lambele*," Ephraim chanted mischievously.

"Like hell you're hungry. Go on, bugger off."

"Christmas box, Boss Kramer?"

"Give you a kick up the arse, if that's any good."

The other angel fled and Ephraim spat scornfully after him.

"My cousin," he explained. "No damn respect. I must go catch him."

Kramer closed the door.

"You surprise me, Lieutenant. I must say, I never for a moment thought I was entertaining friends of yours."

"Hey?"

"Just joking, you understand."

McDonald tried a chuckle and coughed on it.

"Most people know Ephraim," Kramer said, intrigued by the man's agitation. "Smartest seven-year-old in Trekkersburg. Pa killed ma and we got him, but Ephraim can look after himself."

"Certainly novel, a change from the sods making a hell of a row with guitars out of tins. Beats me, though, why coons think they've got to black their faces! Seem to be more of them every year, a bloody pest, get them at home as well as the office. Not that they usually get past Pat Weston. Er, is she back?"

"No," said Kramer. "There's some old dame at the counter."

"Miss Godfrey? That surprises me even more; she's a right battle-ax. Look, wouldn't you like to take a seat?"

"Ta."

McDonald tried to find something to arrange on his desk top, but it was bare apart from the blotter. So he took out his key ring and jangled it.

"Let's say I know now, Mr. McDonald. Was it really worth all the fuss?"

Jangle, jangle.

"Come on, man."

Jangle, jangle.

"Don't play games with me or—"

"That's what I'm interested in, Lieutenant. I mean what can you do?" McDonald said, trying to sound tough. "My brother's a solicitor."

"And mine is in the Special Branch."

What a lovely fib. It put a stop to those bloody things jiggling about.

62

"Shall we start again, Mr. McDonald? Tell me what's on your mind."

"Simply this: you're going to find that there was nothing sinister about Mark's death. He had more to drink than was good for him—and he hardly ever drank, as it was—then did something bloody silly."

"How do you know he had been drinking?"

"I was at the Old Comrades' Club when he came in last night."

"Time?"

"Before nine-forty, because I had to call a client and saw him arrive. It was a surprise, as he didn't often partake, but then it was also bloody hot."

How well Kramer remembered that, but it was best not to lead your witness to start with.

"Uhuh."

"In that heat, you're not counting, are you? Just belting the stuff down, cold as it'll come. Only takes three or four and you're well away without realizing."

"True."

"To be honest, *I* was well away by nine, and in comes Mark, knocked out—even had a nosebleed like kids do when it's over ninety—and before I was taking it in, he was gone."

"Really?"

"Got myself mixed up in a bit of a singsong, carols and all that, round the piano, my back to him, didn't know if it was my own glass half the time, still no one complained, proper rave-up, forgot he was there. Yes, I feel guilty, he'd said he wanted to talk, should have seen him home, but that's all, I've told you the lot."

"Sorry, but you haven't."

A twanging silence. McDonald jerked as the match flame, unwatched, reached his fingers.

"Here," said Kramer, lighting the king-size for him. "Now get back to why you didn't want Pat Weston to tell me about it."

Inhale and exhale, very slowly.

"Paula, Lieutenant—Paula is suffering enough. And there was nothing to his little affair, that I promise."

"With a wife like that . . ."

"That's Pat, I knew it! Little bitch. Paula's one of the best. Gave up a lot for Mark."

"Uhuh?"

"Which is why it bowled me over when he told me. Came for advice, actually, and bloody well got it, silly clot; told him to pack it in, and he did, then and there. Nothing to it."

"But why?"

"I'd put it down to middle age, to the fact he'd never had the guts to speak to a strange woman in his life, let alone chat her up, then along came . . ."

"And he did?"

"Huh, not in a conventional sense, not in the beginning anyway, if ever."

"Then he just slept with her?"

"Good God, no! Never touched her; I asked."

Kramer lit himself a cigarette and wondered if he was going mad.

"Then what's the big deal?"

"Trust. He was breaking his trust, stepping outside the mark, taking chances on tearing Paula apart. He loved her, loved her, see?"

"Except for half an hour a day."

"She'd picked that up, too, had she? Give Pat her due, she belongs with your brother in the SBs!"

That was a dangerous remark, but McDonald was now very worked up. There was ash all over his nice silk shirt and his bow tie banked to the left.

"It's all right, Mr. McDonald. Nothing of this will get back to Mrs. Wallace if, as you say, her husband's death was aboveboard."

"I have your word?"

"Yes. Now the name of this lady, please."

McDonald stood up, decisive.

"I don't know it," he said defiantly. "I don't know where she lives or what she does. You're the detective; you find out."

"Right," said Kramer, knowing the man was lying. "I will."

Just for the hell of it.

SIX

Jabula is a word with more than one meaning in colloquial Zulu: it is used for happiness, and for beer. Now it was also the name of the settlement on the plain below Zondi, and he, for one, was very happy to be there.

From what he could see through the heat shimmer, Jabula was an area of exposed ground marked off into plots by white flags, with a few rows of tin huts and many makeshift dwellings that reminded him of something much neater but the comparison eluded him. He could see very few people moving about on the wind-patterned sand, although a few children played beneath the motionless windmill. The priest must have gone, which would make things easier.

He had decided to repeat his idea of going in on foot, for a car arriving in such a remote place could cause an unhelpful stir. Its tail feather of dust would also be visible for a good mile (he still thought in the old measurements before metrication). So the Anglia was parked out of sight behind him, and everything he needed was about his person: the automatic in its holster, with the safety off; the cuffs hidden in his waistband under his jersey sleeves—he had knotted it around him like an apron reversed; and the long torch, such as travelers commonly carried, in his right hand. He was sure that his clothes, filthy from the journey, would pass muster as castoffs.

Zondi gave his mental picture of the lieutenant a mocking salute, then began the descent. He was careful not to move briskly, but dragged his feet along, keeping his eyes downcast. This meant he let himself in for a small surprise when he reached the first flag marker.

Lifting his gaze, he saw there were, in fact, very many people resident in Jabula—at a guess, well over three hundred, with the only males being either the very old or the very young. He had not spotted the inhabitants before because they were seated in the shade of their homes, silent, motionless in different attitudes. His immediate reaction was instinctive: a prickling along the spine, a tightening of sinew that halted him in his tracks. Then he realized there was nothing ominous in this, for not a head turned to inspect him. These were people lost in themselves and totally listless. He had once seen something of the kind after a whirlwind flattened a township near Kokstad—but that had nothing to do with anything.

"Greetings, my mother."

Zondi had addressed the person closest to him, an old crone squatting beside an iron bed that lay in pieces. She turned toward him. Her pupils were pale blue; she was blind. What a start.

"Greetings. Who speaks?"

"A traveler, mother, Matthew Shabalala. I go to seek work on the farms to the west."

The crone cackled and staggered to her feet. She reached out and caught Zondi's arm before he thought better of it.

"Then your travels will be long and hard, my son. What men there were with us have already left for those parts."

"Perhaps I have good fortune."

"Huh! If so, then *I* will live to see it!"

When she laughed she showed three teeth and no more. Zondi, who felt good manners had their defined limit, pulled away. But she clung fiercely.

"Tell me," she said, "tell me what you see about you—you will not lie like my children!"

At this a bedraggled woman, with breasts like saddlebags, emerged from a hut. She waved a fist.

66

"Be quiet, you old devil! Would you bring shame on us in front of a stranger?"

"*You* be quiet, Dora Dhlamini—you who would lie to her mother in her old age! You who would say there is no room for her bed in the house, that she must sleep on the floor with the children! What nonsense is this? I know, I know—you wish for her to die out here like a dog in the grass!"

"Just you look at my house," Dora demanded of Zondi, who was sick to the stomach at having attracted so much unwelcome attention. Now other people had gathered, so there was no escape—except through being obliging.

He looked at the hut, past the snot-nosed kids in the doorway, and calculated it was twelve feet deep by nine feet wide. It had an earth floor and a tin roof.

"How many, stranger?" asked Dora Dhlamini.

"Inside this place?"

"Yes."

"Maybe four—five," Zondi said, shrugging.

"There is ten!"

"*Hau*, then you are a liar, my sister!"

The crowd growled angrily.

"Ten because I have no man and cannot pay rent. I must look after these children, these orphans, and for that the GG will let me stay. Now you tell her what you see—there is no room for a bed."

There was no need; the old woman's grip had slackened.

"But I heard the GG say that we will like this place," she said. "We are not forced, we come because it is better for us. Nobody forces us yet. . . . Over there, what do you see, Shabalala?"

Crafty, suspecting a trick, she dragged Zondi around.

"Much furniture, my mother—like your bed, in the grass."

"There!" Dora Dhlamini laughed and the onlookers guffawed at Zondi's discomfiture. He jerked himself free, annoyed that he could not reveal the real reason for it. Then he wiped a hand over his mouth.

"Some water?" he asked.

Again the onlookers enjoyed themselves at his expense.

"This is Jabula," one said. "There is no water."

Zondi pointed his torch at the windmill.

"Tomorrow," an old man in the crowd went on. "Tomorrow they bring water on a lorry—that stupid thing cannot work."

"Tomorrow?" echoed another.

While a third scoffed, "Tomorrow tomorrow, you mean, Bobesi."

Zondi refused to be delayed by a tedious argument over the ways of the GG—a slang expression for officialdom taken from trucks with Government Garage registration plates. So he tried a joke of his own.

"*Hau,*" he said. "Can a man not get drunk in Jabula?"

This time the laughter was on his side. He took advantage of it to ask if perhaps any of his kinsfolk were in the settlement, and was told that some Shabalalas had arrived the day before; they were across the other side where the tents stood.

So that was what the makeshifts were; plainly none of their occupants had the faintest idea how to erect one. An assumption fully substantiated when he reached the Shabalalas', which was propped up by everything but the pole.

There a neighbor informed him that Wilhemena Shabalala was away, having gone to buy food.

"So soon?" he queried casually, aware the state provided all voluntary emigrants to the homelands with rations.

"They give us three pounds of mealie meal for three days."

"And?"

"The family is big."

"Where is the store she buys from?"

The neighbor, a sour-faced frump, puffed the flies from her nostrils and pointed vaguely.

"But that is a great distance!" Zondi exclaimed, recalling how long it was since he had noticed the hole in the water tank.

"Where else? If you wait for her, you will wait till the moon comes. But what do you want with her, traveler?"

"Family matters."

He turned his back on her and made a show of viewing the landscape.

His attention was suddenly drawn to a baffling pattern of hundreds of holes on a slight rise to the east.

"What is that?" he asked.

"The GG," the woman replied. "First people die but we cannot dig down. The GG come and then the soldiers; with big bangs they made plenty of graves."

Zondi stamped a foot experimentally and felt the shock of bedrock reach his hip. He wondered what the people planned to plant there. He wondered how long Shabalala's wife would take to get home—and whether the wait was going to be really worth it.

Another neighbor had taken over at the Wallace household in Chestnut Road; it amused Kramer to find the idle rich reduced to shift work. Not rich, exactly, nor idle, but certainly more comfortably inactive than he had been all his life.

"Gee, but I don't know," this new neighbor said, her American accent requiring an adjustment, when he asked to see Mrs. Wallace. "I don't know what the doctor wanted me to do in this respect. But you step inside a minute and I'll call him."

"He's here?"

"I mean on the telephone. He said Paula was to have no visitors, that I had to pull the drapes in her room and let her be."

"Pills?"

"Sedation. Only a half hour back, too."

She closed the door behind him.

"If you're wondering why the maid didn't answer your knock, it's because she's upset that I—"

"Not to worry."

"Come right on through."

Kramer found the living room in much the state he had left it—paper chains hung forlorn from the picture rail and the tree in the corner needed a bigger bucket. Someone had, however, made a pleasing arrangement of plastic holly and greeting cards along the mantelpiece. He remarked upon it.

"Oh, that? It was me. Guess I just can't stand having nothing to occupy my hands."

"Very nice. And very nice of you to be here by her side at a time like this."

"Who? Paula? She'd do the same for me. I mean me and Steve haven't been neighbors all that long, we came in the fall—our fall, that is—but we've formed a real good relationship that I'm going to miss. Steve's on a sabbatical."

Sabbatical? She did not look Jewish.

"Oh, really?"

"Yes, and we've got to take in a few months at the Cape, so it's pack up and go again pretty soon."

Kramer cruised the bookshelves and found what he wanted: a volume with library codes on the spine.

"Mr. Wallace was a big reader?"

"Phenomenal."

"One a day?"

"Easily; the poor guy had chronic insomnia."

Tinkle went a fragile theory or two.

"So you knew both the Wallaces well, lady?"

"Please, I'm Alicia, Alicia Brown. Yes, all four of us were in and out of each other's homes without knocking most of the time."

"Then is it all right if I ask you a couple of questions—save Mrs. Wallace the trouble?"

"Hey, wait a minute. Depends what kind of questions. Our cops don't go through all this for a car smash."

"Maybe not, Mrs. Brown, but we have our own ways of doing things in the Republic. But relax, please; only routine. For a survey we're doing, if you must know—state of mind, et cetera."

"That sounds okay."

"How was he then, yesterday—Mr. Wallace?"

She frowned but stayed pretty, taking it all very seriously. Kramer, who had ignored blond hair on principle since Lisbet, was weakening rapidly. He also liked her smell.

"Now you mention it, not quite himself, I guess."

Poor bastard. Kramer knew the feeling.

"What did you put this down to?"

"His not sleeping, the goddamn awful heat. I was over just after breakfast with the mail, you see; one of theirs landed in our box by mistake. Just a card, so I could have waited, but that's how things were between us. Mark was going through the pile, opening envelopes, and Paula was reading out names, y'know. I kind of busted it up for them, I guess. Still, Paula didn't seem to mind. Went out back to the kitchen to see the cook fixed another coffee for me, and Mark just sat there."

"Oh?"

"Not saying anything, staring. I had to kid him a little before he snapped out of it."

"And then?"

"Made some joke, I forget. He left for the office pretty soon afterwards. Is that what you wanted? Doesn't seem a big deal to me."

It was Kramer's turn to become lost in thought—only he came around on his own.

"And Mrs. Wallace?"

"As always, a honey; chirpy as a chipmunk. Say, would you like some coffee—oops, tea?"

"Coffee's my people's drink, same as yours," Kramer replied, smiling. This was ideal; he wanted her out of the room for a minute. "But the servants are off, you said?"

"It won't bother me, Lieutenant."

Kramer took in all he could of the swing of the fine-pleated skirt and then moved quickly. He took out the library book, artfully eliminated the gap in the row, and pushed his loot into the waistband of his trousers around the back. It was all over in seconds and his posture much improved.

Then he continued around the room, exhibiting the polite curiosity of a visitor admiring good taste, but finding none of the brittle ornaments to his liking. Out of sheer habit, he lifted the top crumpling of paper from the waste bin by the desk—and then hoisted an eyebrow.

A Christmas card, torn into many small pieces, lay at the bottom. He had it out and luckily in his pocket just as Alicia Brown entered silently with the tray.

There was a small shopping center half a mile back from Chestnut Road where Kramer was able to buy a roll of wide adhesive tape and the last copy of the *Trekkersburg Gazette*. Then he drove on to a small park and found some shade. The lawn there was like lawn everywhere in the suburb of Caledon: it was green. This did a lot for his soul. For a time he just looked at it, oblivious to the black nannies gossiping away their afternoon break, and to their little charges snatching at rainbows in the spray of the sprinklers. Grass; there had to be more square yards of good grass per head in Caledon than in the rest of the city put together, and all just for looking at or planting your bum on. Bloody marvelous.

Yet he stayed in the car, as he had now a little work to do. First he checked through the newspaper and saw that the fatality had been reported but without naming names. Fine. Then he began tearing off strips of tape, which he stuck to the car window so each one slightly overlapped, along the lines of a closed slat blind. When he had completed a rectangle about eight inches by six, he stuck more strips at angles across it and built up a backing. Once this was thick enough, he was able to peel the whole lot away and tape it, sticky side up, on his map book cover.

All set, he carefully took out the torn greeting card and spread it over the passenger seat. It did not take a genius to work out that the plain white bits, which of course also had type and ink lines on them, belonged to the inside. He gathered all these together and pushed the others aside. His luck was in: one diamond-shaped scrap had a small *s* on the left, a gap, then a capital *C* on the right: *Kersfees*—gap—*Christmas*. A bilingual card with the two official languages side by side, presupposing they had been centered there by the printer.

Kramer stuck this in the middle of the prepared area and looked for more. Almost immediately he found a very nearly intact *Happy* that fitted above perfectly. Then good fortune gave way to perpetual difficulties and it was an hour before he had got as far as the rest of the

72

manufacturer's trite message: *Happy Christmas and a Prosperous New Year*. But already he had come across something unusual—the word "Prosperous" in the English version had been underlined four times.

This spurred him on to sort out the handwriting section and very soon he had a man's name: *Sam*. Sam Smith? Sam Jones? Sam van der Merwe? That was the jackpot question, but all he had toward it were an *a* on one piece and an *anth* on another. To complicate matters further, the torn edges were so straight they could fit together in almost any order. Damn; he must have missed a few more scraps in that bin. Bugger it.

Unless, of course, there was such a . . .

He called the duty officer on the radio and asked him if there were any messages from Zondi.

"Not a thing, Tromp. You know how these Kaffirs are—probably sleeping it off someplace."

"*Ach*, too true."

"Anything else I can do, hey?"

"And why not? Ever heard of Samantha, Koos?"

"Bing Crosby, wasn't it?"

"Again?"

"I mean he sang it, in a filum. *High Society?* Princess Morocco was the popsy, you remember. Why?"

"I thought maybe you were playing requests this afternoon, that's all. You call this a radio?"

Koos laughed, made a rude nosie, and signed off.

It did not all flood back into Kramer. He disliked visiting the bioscope and disliked Hollywood musicals most of all. But at least he knew now that Samantha was a real name and could carry on from there.

Trying to fit together all of the white pieces was virtually impossible so he simply stuck them down haphazardly and, by noting the area they covered, satisfied himself that nothing of the card was missing.

"Prosperous" underlined and the single word "Samantha"; not a lot there, but Mark Wallace must have thought so. You do not usually tear up Christmas cards, especially if it is your custom to display them.

But Kramer decided to shelve hypothesis and try a shortcut. He had a strong feeling he knew where to find this Samantha, and she could bloody well supply the explanations.

Zondi had decided to spend the time as profitably as possible and dozed off. Food was unnecessary and water could wait, but going without sleep for more than thirty-six hours was another thing: it reduced his state of alertness and made his ears ache. It also impaired his capacity for attention to detail—as he realized upon a rude awakening.

The woman with flies in her nose was kicking at his shoe, calling him names.

"GG spy!" she hissed. "Spy, where are your sticks?"

Zondi sprang to his feet, reassured himself that so far these allegations had not attracted attention, then poked her hard in the voice box with one finger. She gasped and went down in a heap. Nobody noticed. He grabbed her arms and dragged her into her tent. Not a fly followed.

"You say GG one more time and I'll kill you, my sister."

A croak pledged her silence.

"And when you can talk, you will say you are very sorry for this. Have you a man?"

The bowed head managed a shake.

"I will wait."

He was furious. Furious with himself as much as with her, for he should have remembered that nobody would go on a journey without his two hardwood sticks, one for fending off blows and the other for striking. Occasionally you would see a man with a single stick, but certainly never a man empty-handed—just as in cowboy films, where every white man had a revolver. Little wonder her suspicions had been aroused and possibly, as he slept, she had spotted his gun. She was the type not to be frightened by such a discovery but to react with rash indignation. The others he had met earlier had simply been too involved in the argument to notice. Which brought him back to his other reason for anger: the fact that his cover had been destroyed and now he would have to do things the hard way.

He sprawled on a grass mat in the back of the tent, patted his pockets for his cigarettes, and took a light from a box of her matches. The

74

woman, who had been weeping very quietly, tried to edge to the opening.

"Stay. I wish to hear why you think I am a GG spy."

Her first words in reply were lost, then she regained a degree of audibility.

"Shabalala," she whispered. "He comes to Jabula."

Zondi was jolted upright. At last, something to vindicate his actions —something to charge his being with a proper sense of purpose again.

"When is this?"

"In the night."

"Last night?"

"He was with his wife this morning."

"You spoke to him?"

"No."

"You know why he is here?"

"No."

"His wife said nothing?"

"Just asked me not to say to anybody."

"Why not?"

The woman shrugged and began to sob.

"*Why?* You had better answer me—quick!"

"Maybe his pass. GG very strict."

So that was it, and a natural enough assumption on her part to suppose that the policy with regard to the movement of Africans in and out of white areas could make Shabalala's unsanctioned homecoming a hazardous undertaking. Zondi knew that at the stroke of a clerk's pen, a man could be endorsed out of a city in which he was born to a homeland hundreds of miles away—and that this applied even to such a man as the business tycoon who headed an official township council but was officially classified as casual laborer. Yes, it was quite possible she was telling him what she truly thought.

"But I am not GG, I am CID," Zondi said.

"*Hau!*"

"Yes, and this Shabalala is a very bad man. You are not safe with him near to your place."

"In what way?"

Zondi drew a thumb across his throat.

"*Hau!* You must catch him!"

"You must help me."

"I am frightened."

"Then just tell me where he is."

"But he is gone."

"When?"

"Not long ago—just before you come."

And she shrank back terrified as Zondi showed his new rage. For a whole two hours he had slept while the killer made good his escape, no doubt cutting across country and heading for— Now that was a point. Zondi could think of nowhere Shabalala would be better off than back in Jabula. It was the woman's mention of pass books that had brought this to mind. Without the proper papers for traveling, Shabalala had already been very lucky to get so far without being picked up in one of the constant checks made by the uniform branch—and he was unlikely to risk his neck again without good reason. All he had to do was hide until the law had gone.

"My sister," Zondi said, now in friendly fashion. "You say Shabalala goes just before I come. Where does he go?"

"Through this part, up by the huts."

"What was he doing before this? Was he watching that hill?" Zondi nodded his head in the direction of the hidden Anglia.

"He stood outside looking, looking. I see that, but I don't see where he looks."

Shabalala must have looked and seen a stranger approaching who carried no sticks. If only the woman had been even slightly educated, then Zondi could have asked her to estimate the timing more exactly; but she had lived all her life without knowing that time was divisible, like a bowl of porridge between her children, into a number of small and exact parts. Still, there were other ways.

"Shabalala goes and I come," he said. "Between these two things happening, what did you do? Fold your blankets? How many blankets?"

"That I did this morning."

"But you understand my question."

"I did nothing. What is there to do in this place? Should I clean the dirt from the dirt?"

Perhaps schooling would have been quite the wrong thing for her and the world had been spared much trouble. Zondi despised those of his people who could not stay proud.

"No. Clean your nostrils, my sister."

She spat, so she despised him, too. At least she was Zulu enough to have courage—and that he could respect.

He laughed and she laughed and then it was time to begin the search. It had occurred to him that the old crone who waylaid him just might have been part of a deliberate attempt to divert the course of justice.

seven

Kramer was hurrying past the Albert Hotel when he remembered he had agreed to meet Scott there at five. It was ten after the hour according to the clock on Trekkersburg City Hall. He turned back and pushed his way into the saloon bar.

It was so crowded with jolly businessmen bracing themselves to play Santa that another three minutes had to be added to his apology when he finally found the lieutenant drinking orange squash.

"Hell, man, but I'm sorry," he said.

"Think nothing of it. What's yours?"

"Not now, hey."

"Pardon?"

"Look, John, I'll be back in a sec—must hurry before it closes."

"What?"

Kramer felt he had slipped up, but improvised glibly.

"The shop, of course. Present."

"You'd better run then, man—and don't worry, I'll wait."

A certain sourness on Scott's face could not be missed. Kramer quite enjoyed having put it there.

He hastened back into the street and found himself shoulder deep in closing-time shoppers moving at the speed of the frailest legs among them. His immediate attempt to reach the roadway and dodge through the traffic jam was frustrated by the sheer weight of numbers packed so tightly together. One thing was for sure: every beggar, all the way down to the post office, had long since crawled away to avoid being trampled to mush. There was good in everything if you looked for it.

"Excuse," he said, trying to barge through the crush sideways.

"Watch it, son!" snapped an old turtle, lifting his scaly bald head from its tweed jacket shell. "Let's have some manners while we're about it."

"Murder Squad," Kramer replied, and won an advance of two yards before being trapped again.

"Murder Squad," said Kramer.

"It is," grumbled a fat lady who had set up a human barrier on either side of her by having her four kids hold hands. "And my feet, they're murder, too."

Christ, this was how a germ must feel, the way Doc Strydom described it, when trying to get down a vein with all those bloody cells having a go. What an inspired thought.

"I am a doctor!" Kramer said with considerable success—and he kept saying it as often as was necessary until he reached the library steps. A notice pinned over the schedule on the notice board announced that it was closing at six, earlier than usual for a weekday, but that borrowers would be welcome till then.

He took out the book lifted from the Wallace house and went in. Not surprisingly, there were few members of the public about; mostly pensioners trying to find themselves a little Christmas cheer that was free, something to occupy their minds in lieu of their stomachs. Very sad.

But the entire staff seemed to be present and quite animated for a change. Several of the women actually had a bright color discreetly positioned on their dresses, and one had undone her bun. Then he noticed, through the glass doors to the junior section, which had closed at four, the low tables covered with eats and glasses. Of course; they were all set for a wild party, at the height of which the head librarian would distribute banned books he had withdrawn, each in its pretty gift wrappings. The consequences were unimaginable—if the censors knew their job.

Cinderella, however, did not look as if she was going to make this ball. She stood a little behind the two dumpy ladies dealing briskly with an old couple's returned books, her face hidden by long blinkers of soft straight hair. It was bright black hair, in the same way a gun barrel could be bright black, and made a sharp contrast with the coarse weave of her smock.

Kramer hesitated and looked around for something more like what he was after. But a sharp remark from one of the others had the girl come forward to take the book.

"But this . . ." she said.

"Yes, miss?"

"Nothing."

She opened it to show its date-stamp insert and then began picking through the wide tray of card holders on the counter. She found the right one and pulled out a card that had on it in block letters: MR. M. C. WALLACE, 9 CHESTNUT ROAD, CALEDON, TREKKERSBURG, and in printing: "For Fiction Only. This Card Cannot Be Transferred."

That brought her head up, too fast for the hair, and Kramer could see she was wishing she could turn into a pumpkin. He was also aware of looking at a girl who was, in her very own way, not pretty but possibly beautiful. He had never been sure about these things since meeting the Widow Fourie.

"What's the matter, miss?"

"I— You aren't who it says here."

"No? You know all your customers, hey?"

She went red.

"My name's Kramer, miss. And yours?"

"Sa—"

Almost, but not quite, an automatic response; it showed she had control of herself.

"Then I'll take a guess: Samantha?" But she turned from him.

"Miss Finlay, please," the girl called to a colleague, turning, her voice lower than she had expected it to be.

"Don't do that, Samantha—not if you don't want a fuss," Kramer warned softly.

"*Who are you?*" she whispered.

"A police officer, and I want a quiet little chat. Are you going to the party?"

"No."

"Then I'll be outside at six, on the steps. If you're a sensible girl, you won't try to leave by the back."

"Can I be of assistance, Miss Simon?" cut in the same woman who had been a busybody before.

Samantha Simon. The two names went together very nicely.

"It's all right, thank you, Miss Finlay."

But the busybody was only getting started.

"Some little difficulty, Mr. Wallace?" she inquired abruptly, cheating at cards and getting caught.

"*Ach*, no, lady. I'm from the police—see?" Kramer sighed, showing her his identification card but keeping a thumb over "Murder Squad."
"Some kind bloke finds your book lying on a bus. This bloke brings it to us. The charge office hears I'm going this way. I hand it in."

"That's all right then."

"Which is what I said, Miss Finlay."

"Why the fuss though, Miss Simon?"

"No fuss," she said, staring in emphasis across to Kramer.

"Happy Christmas, ladies," he said, and left.

Zondi identified himself properly to the inhabitants of Jabula as an arm of the law—one with a Walther PPK nine-millimeter automatic pistol conveniently near the end of it. Perhaps there was some risk in displaying the weapon, but it was a quick way of convincing a largely illiterate crowd of skeptics that he was what he claimed to be. Conviction did not, however, bring with it cooperation. Only the potbellied children, excited out of their lethargy, were eager to do as he asked. The rest glowered from doorways or impeded the search, moving about incessantly, so it was quite possible for Shabalala to keep changing his hiding place.

While the mob's behavior exasperated Zondi, it also served to reinforce his suspicion that Shabalala was somewhere very close at hand.

And, when he finally blew his top, it took no less than two shots into the air to clear everybody from where the huts and tents stood.

Zondi made them all stand on the other side of a line between two white flags, and then threatened to shoot anyone who crossed over. As he could not see to this order being obeyed and carry out the search simultaneously, he called up his child auxiliaries and offered a bounty of ten cents to the one who first spotted Shabalala.

The mothers watched dull-faced as their small sons and daughters scampered back into the living quarters, shrieking merrily as they invaded other people's privacy. The old blind woman started wailing: the whole world had gone mad, and she was going to step over the line and end it all. When her daughter angrily offered to point her in the right direction, she shut up again. Meanwhile, the woman who had the flies back on her sores tried to impress upon the people around her that the fugitive was a dangerous man—a killer. Those who troubled to listen were left apparently unmoved.

After ten minutes or so, the children began to drift back. One had sugar on its face and another a bulge in the cheek.

"Look!" a grizzled-haired old man suddenly cried out in horror. "Our food! The children have been taking the food!"

Zondi snatched out his pistol and leveled it at him.

For even before the first anguished words, he realized he had made the worst mistake of his life by sending in the children. Potbelly, empty belly—it was an old saying. And youngsters had no idea of tomorrow, they did not understand rationing, nor had they learned to ignore the gnaw of hunger. Let them see food and they grabbed it—provided no adult was there to prevent them. It had been like inviting a swarm of locusts to find ten cents' worth of grain hidden in a wheat field.

"We shall starve! Starve!"

"Stay back!"

But the people were beginning to move toward Zondi, taking up the old man's cry of starvation, and waving their fists. They were no longer afraid. The gun was a quick death; what they faced now was slow and terrible.

"Back, or I shoot!"

They came on. All their pent-up frustration, their bewilderment, their anger focused on this one man—this maniac who had already virtually destroyed them.

"*Bulala! Bulala!*"

The three most dreaded syllables in the ears of any lone policeman —the Zulu chant for "Kill!" Once uttered, the word was an incantation that totally banished fear and replaced it with a wild blood lust only bullets could halt—if you had enough of them. Zondi had four.

"*Bulala, bulala, bulala!*"

The tempo was increasing and the front rank of the mob was twenty yards away. The shadow of a stone grazed Zondi's gun hand. Keeping calm was fine, but had its limitations. If they reached him, he could count on killing four, perhaps five with a lucky shot close up. This would still leave him with something like over two hundred fifty berserk women. They would assuredly tear him apart with their hands and their teeth. Four rounds. He could fire three and use the other on himself. He could try and reach a child to use as a hostage, but that would not necessarily stop them. He could run.

Zondi aimed suddenly at the tail vane of the windmill, pulled the trigger, and the bullet ricocheted loudly. The musical sound was unexpected: it made heads turn on reflex.

He ran.

Surprisingly, Scott had not been unduly put out when Kramer came back to say all the shops had shut so he would have to go down to the Indian quarter for the present.

"Trust the bloody *churras* to be Mohammedan," Scott grunted. "Do anything to keep their shops open."

"So you don't mind?"

"I'm having a loaf, aren't I? Besides, Colonel Dupe knows where I am if anything comes up."

Which went some of the way toward explaining the plain orange juice.

"Nothing so far from Zondi?" Kramer asked casually.

"Nothing. Looks like he decided to knock off early for Christmas."

"*Ach*, who knows?"

Kramer gave a nod and left the Albert Hotel once more, heading for the library. This time the streets were almost deserted, which allowed him to concentrate on wondering just what had really become of that crazy black bastard. On past performances, Zondi would have been back with his prisoner by now—or would have at least telephoned in to report developments. Kramer hoped fervently he had not gone and done something stupid.

Samantha Simon backed out through the library doors, thanking the head librarian for thinking of her, but insisting she had to get home. Then she turned to find Kramer right there.

"My place or yours?" he said.

"Pardon?"

"Where are we going to have our little chat? My office down at CID?"

Talk about an initial response. The mention of his office dilated her nostrils like the thrust of two thick fingers.

"But what's this all about?"

"First things first. Where? You've got a flat near here, haven't you?"

"Me? No, miles away. In Greenside."

"Very swanky."

"It's only an old servant's room."

"Then I know a place where it's quiet," Kramer said, steering her abruptly down an alleyway leading into the legal quarter. Right between the chambers of two eminent advocates was a small tearoom which flourished on a lunchtime trade of forensic take-aways. The sign in the window was showing CLOSED, yet the door finally opened to Kramer's loud knocking.

"Lieutenant, what a pleasure!"

The smarmy creep who ran it ushered them in and then went behind his counter. Plastic holly was melting on the top of his espresso coffee contraption, and it stank.

"A little late to call, perhaps, and it is Christmas Eve, of course, but a pleasure all the same," the creep said. "What is it to be?"

"Two coffees, black, put sugar and milk on the table."

"But that's no way for me to treat an honored guest, Lieutenant!"

"You're on fire."

"Oh, I'm most terribly sorry."

The creep removed the decoration from the machine, gratifyingly burning his fingers in the process.

"Tough luck," said Kramer. "Hurry up with those bloody coffees, then push off."

"Anything you say, Lieutenant."

The coffees, the milk, and the sugar were put down with great care before them. Then the proprietor made for the rear door, leading to his flat.

"I said push off, Gordon. You want me to put it differently in front of a lady?"

"But—but where?"

"Out. In the street. And don't come back till that says 'Open.' "

"I must say this seems a bit of a liberty."

"Nothing like the one you take with certain matters, shall we say, overheard on these premises? Sam Safrinsky still wants to know how news of his surprise witness got to Oosthuizen."

"You're not suggesting—"

"I'm saying. Now go."

Samantha had sat stiff and quick-eyed through this exchange, one which Kramer had contrived more for its effect on her than on sulky Gordon, now clicking away indignantly on elevator shoes.

"Relax," he said to her affably. "I'm only like that if I think somebody's trying fast ones on me. Milk?"

She took hers black and without sugar. Took a small sip and did not relax at all.

"I wish to interview you in connection with a certain Mr. Mark Wallace," Kramer began. "You have been associating with Mr. Wallace over a period, and this association—"

"How do you know?"

"Simple. It was a fact that there was another woman involved, but nobody could understand how Wallace could see her in only half an hour a day, during which time he also changed his library books. This suggested one of two things to me. The first was that he got his lady friend to change his books for him earlier in the day, and he picked them up when he saw her. But then one of his friends said that he was not the sort of bloke to go talking to strange women. I wondered what women in his life were not quite strangers, might have something in common, as you say. That's why I put the two together and came up with yourself."

"With me? Why not one of the others?"

"You're young and pretty."

"Pah!"

Kramer stirred his coffee, trying to decide whether her laugh was as bitter as the muck he had been given to drink. He decided it was. But did nothing.

"Can I ask you something? What right have you got to bring me here?"

"Now don't start that nonsense, Samantha, because there could be a serious charge, you know."

"Adultery?"

Again a laugh—without sugar.

"So that is what's on your mind, girlie? How many times?"

"You must be joking! Adultery? Where? In the Romance section between *F* and *K*?"

Kramer's laugh was pure amusement, sired by surprise: these modern girls.

"No, I didn't reckon on action on weekdays—but nobody's said anything about weekends to me yet. That's what I've put money on."

Samantha bit her lip. She was now waxing mildly emotional. Good.

"Weekends? I don't know what he even looks like at weekends—I've never seen him then. And—and if you want the truth, I'll tell you something else."

"Go on."

"The bastard's never touched me."

Then she leaned forward over her coffee, hiding behind that bloody hair again. The shoulders alone betrayed she was sobbing.

"I see. Plutonic love, was it?"

This made her mix in a giggle and Kramer was buggered if he saw why. Perhaps hysteria lurked in the offing. He had better get back to the facts.

"I mentioned a charge, Miss Simon, a serious charge, but you have not inquired as to its exact nature. Do I take it that you already know what it could be?"

"No, I don't. I don't care."

"Like that, is it?"

"Yes."

"Since?"

"Since he . . ."

"Dropped you? Said he'd had enough? Went back to wifey? Is that the story?"

"Not the way he tells it."

"Oh, no?"

"I mean we really had something going there, something special. You know what he said? Said he couldn't *afford* it!"

"In what sense?"

"Exactly! That's what I asked."

Samantha tossed her hair aside and looked Kramer full in the face. Now she was angry, really mad.

"He said he couldn't afford to mess up people's lives—meaning hers, of course! But what he really meant was he couldn't afford to lose his job and his ticky-tacky house and his all-American phallic symbol!"

"His what?"

"Car."

Dear God, it had sounded much worse to Kramer, but then English was a dirty language at the best of times.

"In other words, Miss Simon, you're saying he'd rather have his money and his comforts than run away with you?"

"Of course he would. Said the scandal in this dump of a town would finish him, he'd have to start again somewhere else, probably even without references. And at his age."

"I was coming to that myself."

"Then that just shows what sort of person you are. We loved each other, he was a bit older, so what?"

"Loved? Not love?"

"What do you think?"

"*Ach*, well, you know, like you say, I'm that sort of person."

She snorted, amused.

"You think I might still love Mark? Well, you're wrong. Now I love *myself*, see?—and hate what he's done to me!"

"All without using his hands?"

"Christ. You'd never understand."

She stood up and he thought he would have to tell her to sit down again, but she only wanted more coffee. She helped herself.

"Try me, Miss Simon. Tell me all about it."

"Why have you gone off the Samantha bit? Technical reason, Lieutenant?"

"I don't want you getting overexcited."

"Oh, really? You're quite human in your way, aren't you? I thought the SAP preferred monsters with no necks plus hair on their biceps."

"*Ach*, then I'm a master of disguise. Ta."

She had refilled his cup as well.

"From where do I start?"

"From where he came into your life."

"On a Monday morning when I was tidying Science Fiction. We saw each other through the case over the top of the fourth row. He was on the other side, New Fiction, and it happened just with the eyes. Don't ask me what *it* was; it just was."

"Then?"

"I wondered all week whose eyes it had been, felt a fool because it all reminded me of one of those ghastly nursing stories—a nurse in the operating room who never saw under a junior surgeon's mask till she—oh, you know."

"Uhuh."

"Then I was stamping books out on Friday and there they were—and I knew his name from the card. I made some remark about his choice of reading and he went all shy and shot off."

"Back on the dot Monday?"

"He was. Combing the shelves for a title that would make me say something. Told me later. He chose *Inorganic Chemistry, Part III*, by the way."

"Uhuh."

"Well, don't you think that was funny? Never mind. Then the titles became a bit more, well, *pointed*, you could say, and he asked me if I'd read any of them. To cut a long story short, we talked a lot about books and naturally said a lot about ourselves."

"And the queue at the counter, meantime? How about Miss Finlay?"

"Bitch. Oh, no. By now we had a regular meeting place up in the gallery. Nobody much likes putting those books back, so it wasn't hard to get myself landed with the job most days. And that's all."

"Hey?"

"You don't have to *do* anything to have a love affair, do you? It is or it isn't. Anyway, I thought it was just a beginning—that he'd sort himself out, be honest with himself, stuff convention. I thought it would work out because it was *right*. Know what I mean?"

If he did not, the Widow Fourie undoubtedly could. Only she had decided their little arrangement was not right. Had packed up and off to the Cape.

Kramer slipped back into context and put his feet up on a tabletop.

"What happened to change your mind, Samantha?"

"*My* mind? Hell! Mark's, you mean. I suspected something when he started some nonsense about being watched, only I pushed it aside."

"Hey?"

"He said, all of a sudden one morning, that a man had his eye on us from the gallery over the other side."

"Did you see this man?"

"There was one, but minding his own business, need I add. Anyway, Mark and I were not what you might call getting to grips with one another. I was up the ladder."

"Showing leg?"

Kramer's insight was perfect but his timing terrible. She stopped bending straws and frowned. Then smiled.

"Well, do you blame me?"

"Like hell," Kramer said, throwing in an ogle.

"Then of course the same man has to be there the next day and Mark saw him."

"Private detective?"

"God, I'd never thought of that!"

"Mark probably did."

This made her quiet for a time, then anger began to feed into her fingers, making her twist the straws viciously and break them.

"He told you he'd have to pack it in, Samantha? Said he couldn't afford it and all that?"

"That's right, the bastard. I hate him—hate him."

"For what he did to you?"

"And to himself! God, if only he'd let himself go he could really be something—live, be alive! Instead . . ."

"You really don't think he meant what he said about his wife?"

"How could he?"

"It's possible."

"Rubbish."

"You're a youngster still, Samantha. You may come to—"

"Don't you start that bloody nonsense with me! Just you don't! Oh, my God, I could kill him!"

"Interesting," said Kramer, as she flung herself through the door to the Ladies.

But hardly surprising. All the classic angles of the three-sided figure were there, and one of its sharp points had cut open this little girlie's heart. If she did not come back out of the bog in two minutes, he would have to break down the door.

She was back in under ninety seconds, pretty pert and showing she was the other sort, the kind that cauterizes a wound with hot hate and fights on. Or so she was trying to make herself believe—possibly by taking certain lines of action, innocent in terms of physical violence but as nasty as a bomb out of a blue sky. The trouble was that excess emotionalism often led to the consequences being overlooked; an atomic blast for the sake of the bang, with not a thought for the shock wave or fallout. And Samantha Simon was standing right in the way of some fallout at that very moment, unaware of what her amateur Nagasaki had yet to do to her.

"I'd like to go now—I've told you everything. You can ask him the rest."

"That he prefers being well off to love in one room in Greenside?"

"Yes; ask him."

"Then just one more question, miss. I want you to take a look at something I've got here."

She came over to the table and perched on the edge of her chair, making it plain she would be detained only a moment or so.

Kramer drew out the reconstituted Christmas card and slid it across.

"This arrived in the post at the Wallaces' house yesterday morning," he said. "Does it bear your name?"

"It—but it isn't . . ."

"And can you tell me what word is underlined on this card?"

"Pros—prosperous?"

"That's right; you wish him a prosperous new year. A year with lots of money. In other words, a year when he can *afford* what he likes. But not his little library assistant."

"I—did—not—send—this—card," Samantha said quietly, each word spoken with separate emphasis. She had gone white, bright white the way a decapitated corpse goes.

Kramer shook his head.

"Sorry, Samantha; that's not how I see it."

Now she was trembling, trying to stand.

"All right: what is this about?"

He shrugged.

"What's the charge?"

"No charge."

"I—I can go?"

Kramer waved a hand at the door. Her eyes went narrow, her mouth curled into a small sneer.

"And no punishment?"

"*Ach,* read about it in the papers."

"Don't be funny."

Funny? He was being hilarious. The day after Boxing Day, the *Trekkersburg Gazette* would have the full details of the fatal accident—including the name Mark Clive Wallace. In three days, to put it another way, Samantha Simon would know what despair can do to a man pushed too far. The line of print would jerk like a rope.

But there was good in everything. Kramer was now free to give old Zondi a hand.

eight

Zondi lay bleeding into his handkerchief on the hill overlooking Jabula. A sharp flint had torn into his temple as he fled the mob, another stone had done something bad to his back, but otherwise he was at least still in one piece.

In the moonlight the distance he had run seemed far shorter than it had been. He noted the dried-up stream where most of his pursuers had dropped back, exhausted. He realized with a shudder that the remainder, who must have been recent arrivals, and still in good condition, had almost reached the slope before stopping, too. They were the bastards who had thrown the stones in a desperate bid to bring him down. Now there was nobody out in the veld and no sign of life except for the flicker of a few fires.

The wound hurt, but in no way approximated the pain he felt deep inside: the pain of his failure. Now it would take a hundred armed policemen to get anywhere near Jabula—and every one of those hundred would inevitably come to hear of how he, Mickey Zondi, had run, tail between his legs, from a crowd of shouting women. Never mind what the truth of the matter had been; the joke would soon spread to the farthermost station. And when the laughter reached the ears of the lieutenant, that would be the finish of Mickey Zondi, whatever had gone before.

Zondi had not made any effort to leave the hill, simply because he could think of nowhere to go. The thought of driving back to Miriam had crossed his mind, but lasted no longer than it took to picture himself explaining what had happened. Also, the children might overhear, for all the family slept in the same small room.

He smiled thinly. It seemed now, ironically, that he and Shabalala shared a dilemma—they were both fugitives from the law, both without a sanctuary, both without hope this side of the grave. The only peace they would ever find was in, yes, death. Deep in a grave where the earth was moist and no sound could penetrate the sun-baked crust. Deep, deep down.

He looked across at the graves on the far slope, testing the authenticity of his unfamiliar mood, seeing if he really felt unable to live on with the cross of what he had done. It was in such times, he acknowledged with self-disgust, that weak men return to the God-talk of their childhood and remember words such as "cross." As it happened, his feelings remained unchanged by an appraisal of the graveyard. That, in a strange way, made him feel stronger. At least strong enough for one more squeeze on the trigger. He had three bullets left.

Two too many, while Shabalala would have none. The man would find a tree and tie his belt to it. Put the belt around his neck and slip from the branch. Die with his eyes staring and his tongue sticking out at the moon. A little later, his bowels would open and empty themselves down his trouser legs. As the lieutenant had often said, a noose was the world's best laxative. As the lieutenant . . .

But this was nonsense. Shabalala would not want to die; they would have to tie him to a stretcher with the sixty or seventy other condemned men in the big cell looking on, singing their hymns, waiting their turn.

Zondi's injuries were making him feverish; soon he would not be able to think straight, to do what had to be done. He took the pistol from under his arm and felt the brute weight of it.

His eyes moved back to the graves, calculating from the grid pattern how many had already been filled in, and then beginning, but not completing, a count of the open holes. Black holes, secret holes, open-mouthed for their single ration of man. They did not frighten him. He wanted a place where he could—

The pistol slipped from Zondi's hand. His taut body sagged. Light blazed in his mind, leaving him exalted.

"Shabalala!" he said out aloud, snapping his fingers, cheerfully cursing himself, feeling on top of the world and no pain.

The graveyard was a perfect place in which to hide.

Colonel Du Plessis was also at the Albert Hotel when Kramer finally turned up for his drink with Scott. The two of them were standing at the bar against the wood paneling on the far side. They gave him broad smiles and raised glasses of lager. Thank God for that, if nothing else. Orange juice, for Christ's sake!

"Well, what did you get her, Tromp?"

"Something nice."

"And delivered it in person, too, hey?" asked the Colonel, very snide.

Kramer looked down at him and, just for an instant, enjoyed a quickie fantasy in which he beat the old bitch to her knees with a brick. Then he chuckled and got an elbow on the counter.

Paul Rampaul, the most excellent of all Indian barmen, placed a brandy concoction beside it without a second lost. It was said that Paul, an urbane, very handsome man of considerable natural dignity, knew the favorite drink of every one of his customers—and proved this on their second visit.

"Merry Christmas, Paul."

"And to you, Mr. Kramer, sir. A pleasure to see you again."

That was all. None of the obsequious stuff most Indian barmen traded in. Mr. Rampaul was already back polishing his glasses.

"And how goes the Wallace case, Tromp?" asked Scott.

"Fine. I've got it all wrapped up."

"Oh, dear, does that mean I've got to read your report now, Lieutenant?"

"I'll give it to you verbal, sir."

"Please, not tonight. Anyway, I like—"

"Everything on paper?"

The Colonel caught the edge of Kramer's remark and specks of ice froze in his watery eyes. Every now and then, there was a tiny glimmer of evidence to support the myths surrounding this meek little whiner—this wormlike snake with fangs an inch long. But Kramer had never been one to bother with historic precedent.

"Yes, everything down on paper, my friend. I want everything—post-mortem, laboratory tests, scene of accident, statements."

"*Lab tests*, Colonel?"

"I said that, didn't I, Lieutenant Scott?"

Scott squirmed, then saw Kramer's wink.

"Yes, sir, you said that."

"But hell, Colonel, man, it's an open-and-shut!" Kramer objected. "Wallace got on the booze at the Comrades' because of the heat, wasn't used to holding his liquor, came down the hill too fast and couldn't make it. Chucked his arms up to protect himself and bam."

"Kramer!"

"Sir?"

"That report will be on my desk at HQ on Boxing Day at ten sharp. Understood?"

"But, sir, I thought that as—"

"You think nothing once I've given an order!"

The other customers—and there were still a good number of errant fathers and husbands working themselves up to take knife to turkey—had paused in their joke-swapping about wife-swapping to eavesdrop. Paul Rampaul had discreetly left for the kitchen across the yard.

"Isn't the lab closed over Christmas, Colonel?" said Kramer, keeping his voice calm.

"*Ach*, so it is!" the Colonel replied, becoming instantly jolly. "Send your stuff down to Durban—they're open—and we'll make that the day after Boxing Day—Friday. But I'll have the rest of it when I said."

"I'm to work Christmas Day?"

"Never know you to miss one, Lieutenant. It's true, you know, Scott, this is a dedicated officer we have with us."

So Kramer had been right—the bastards were out to get him. And

Scott was already on the other side—very sly with his meaningful glances at the Colonel, very careful to laugh in the right places. But such positive proof of their intentions was unexpected. Perhaps the lager had something to do with it. No, unlikely. Whatever these men were, they were not given to carelessness. It gave the whole thing a new, vaguely sinister twist.

The lull in the exchange had encouraged their audience to get back to the one about the chap who came home unexpectedly and found a baboon in his closet.

"May I get you another, Mr. Kramer?"

"Thank you, Paul."

"Maybe you think I'm being an old woman," said the Colonel, nudging Kramer in the ribs. "Point is—and you must have overlooked this —I'm on temporary duty as divisional commandant. Colonel Muller gets back from the Free State on Friday lunchtime and I want all my own business tidied up by then for the handing-over ceremony."

"Sir."

"*Ach*, don't think I can't see you are disappointed, Tromp. I know what you were wanting to do: to give your little black friend some help on the Swart case."

"Black what, sir?"

"*Ach*, you must have more faith in him, man!"

"I'll try, sir."

The Colonel and Scott both laughed loudly, as if Kramer had meant to be witty. So he pretended he had, forsaking his sarcasm.

"Come on, gentlemen, this round's on me," he said. "What is it to be?"

They had one drink with him, during which time he learned there still was no news from Zondi, then they left together. What bastards.

"Paul?"

"Mr. Kramer?"

"Here's ten rand. Tell me when I owe you more."

"I . . ."

"Yes, Paul? Speak up, man."

"I have no right to say anything, Mr. Kramer."

Paul's expression was very troubled as he pressed the glass up for the first of the doubles.

How Zondi had taken so long to arrive at the obvious was more than he could understand. Right back at the start he had realized that Jabula itself offered poor cover, but with exposed ground all around, it was better than nothing. He had tied himself down to the idea of finding Shabalala on the ground somewhere—or even up in the air, for he had checked the windmill—but never underneath it. While all the time, below the surface was the only place you could hide in a barren flatland. In fact, he could have come to thinking along the right lines much sooner if only he had simply paid proper attention to the fly woman. She had said that Shabalala had walked off through the huts. All Zondi need have done was to follow in his footsteps and then, at the end of the huts, he would have seen the graveyard ahead of him. But no, he had decided Shabalala was somewhere in those huts and had begun his search without asking a single question, convinced that any answer he received would be a lie.

All this was, however, behind him now as he stalked stealthily down on the burial place. There was a chance that Shabalala was no longer there, but this was unlikely, for his wife still had not returned and, if he had ears at all, he would know that the people of Jabula had good reason to deeply resent his coming. He could easily become their next victim.

Zondi refused to consider the chance that he was wrong yet again and Shabalala had never been in the graveyard. That way lay despair; besides, it lacked logic.

He had about a quarter of a mile to go and the grass was very short. There was nothing for it but to get right down and crawl on his elbows. Not only was it important that he should avoid flushing out his quarry; he also had to deceive any watching eye at Jabula: he doubted that his head, let alone his legs, could take another hasty retreat so soon.

Some of the ache and pain had returned, yet it was muted by fresh hope and the sense of well-being inherent in every hunt, whether for man or for beast. Zondi was not quite certain which of the two he would soon encounter skulking in its hole.

His hand touched cold scales and whipped back. *Snake.* Dead snake. He sobbed once with relief. In the dark, without sticks, he could have died then.

Zondi waited, however, for the moon to come out properly from behind cloud to make sure that the thing, a long, dull gleam of cobra, was beyond harming him. It was not uncommon for a snake chopped in half by a spade to still bite the gardener's foot. No, it was quite, quite dead, and he tugged at its tip.

Then he crawled on with his torch between his teeth, trying to ignore what all this was doing to his clothes. There was not much farther to go.

At last he was beside a mound of stone in which a plank cross stood at an angle, just like on the church roof at Robert's Halt. He waited stock still, listening, scoffing silently at the childish prickle of fear induced by such a place. In his job he had learned that a man need fear only the living. But there was no denying it, the smell of death was in the air, and it was never pleasant to breathe.

Not a single sound.

Zondi moved forward, down the rows of the recent dead, and on until he reached the first of the open graves. He lay flat and peered over the edge. It was empty. Six feet deep with sheer sides and a credit to the army engineers' striving to bring perfection to everything.

Just then Zondi heard a pebble fall. It could have been dislodged by a rat, of course. Then a cough.

A wheezing cough that came from somewhere to his left.

Chill air came down into the valley, making the weeds stir uneasily and an owl lift like a shadow from a child's grave. Zondi shivered, mainly because he was sweating heavily.

This was his moment of truth—as the lieutenant would say. Right, Lieutenant, sir, here he comes; let me show you how to get a man out of a six-foot hole without exposing yourself to any danger.

Another cough pinpointed the exact spot. Shabalala was at the near end of the open grave that had a thistle growing beside it. In less than a minute of extreme caution but, more importantly, silent movement, Zondi was there, too.

He raised his head and looked back at Jabula. One fire remained, its glow unbroken by figures seated around it. All were asleep.

Now, Lieutenant!

The dead snake was dropped into the grave, landing on something soft.

In seconds it was over. Shabalala gasped and came up out of the earth like a terrified rabbit out of a viper pit. He made one mighty leap, clawed frantically at the edge of the grave—for he was not a big man—and heaved himself out. He was still on hands and knees when the cuffs went on him and the muzzle of the PPK pressed into his forehead.

"Make no sound," whispered Zondi. "Or I will shoot."

And for the first time that day he prayed—prayed he would not have to pull the trigger.

Paul Rampaul risked his reputation and served a tonic water to Kramer. For a moment or two, it could have gone either way. Then Kramer sipped a little.

"Such is life, Paul."

"Your change, Mr. Kramer."

He slid over the best part of three rand.

"Take half for the kiddies, man."

"That is generous, sir."

"*Ach*, then buy your wife a present!"

Paul took the money with a small, grateful smile; he did not earn much despite the hours he worked. It was a few minutes before closing and only a very drunk bachelor, who lived in the hotel, shared the large room with them. But only in the most marginal sense.

"Quite a night, Paul?"

"Not too bad, sir."

"But trouble in the public bar, I hear. What did old man Hall do? Hell, remember the time that farmer got stroppy in here with a bloke, wanted to start a fight? Then old Hall comes in with his bagpipes going like stuck pigs and they just stood, mouths like this."

Kramer demonstrated and Paul Rampaul chuckled, shaking his head.

"Never fails, Mr. Kramer."

"Well, did he?"

"Took his mouth organ, sir. Doesn't like to risk his pipes in the public. He bought them in Scotland, they say."

"Oh, yes?"

"Will you want another tonic, sir?"

"I'll run you home if you like, man. No hurry."

"It's all right, sir, thank you; I sleep on the premises tonight."

"*Ach*, that's a shame."

"Such is life, sir—your own words."

Kramer was aware that he was talking to this black bugger in much the way he talked to a blacker bugger called Zondi and that this was causing some embarrassment. He did not give a bugger, as it happened. Christmas comes but once a year.

"No, not a tonic, just one more brandy, a single."

"Very good, sir."

Paul set it down before him.

"What shop did you get the present, Mr. Kramer? I believe you went down to my part of the town."

"Huh! That I should remember!"

"May I ask who it was for, sir?"

"Me."

"Sir?"

"My birthday," said Kramer, toasting himself. "Today, the twenty-fourth of December. You should say 'Happy returns.'"

"My best wishes, sir."

Paul Rampaul was unbuttoning his white jacket.

"Not a good day for a birthday, Paul. No bastard's going to give two presents; no, sir."

"Must have been hard as a child, Mr Kramer. Hard to take."

"It was."

By now the barman had changed into his sports jacket and had moved over to switch off the lights.

"I was born," said Kramer, "in Bethlehem. Bloody Bethlehem. Know where that is?"

"Um, yes, sir. A small town in the Orange Free State."

"A *dorp*, not a town. A bloody *dorp*. Let me tell you something."

Paul Rampaul hesitated at the switches, then came across.

"You see, man, my pa, he was a small farmer. A very religious man, too, and every Sunday we were kept sitting in that church, morning and afternoon. They are a religious people up there."

"Really, sir?"

"So bloody religious that when the doc says to my pa that the way things look I'm going to be born on the twenty-fifth, he takes certain steps."

There was a bump from behind them as the bachelor guest used a cushion shot off the wall to get himself through the doorway.

"Like I was saying, he takes steps. First he makes my ma walk up and down half the bloody night to shake me out. But I'm inside, hanging on like a bugger. So next he gets the old *gamaat* to harness the donkeys to the cart and then drive her up and down the bad road to the dam. Still they can't shift me. You know what he does next?"

His listener leaned forward, giving the lie to the belief that they all had curry on their breath.

"He makes the *gamaat* take a horse and bring back a bloody witch doctor! Honest, that's sodding truth! Tells the old baboon that he'd better give my ma the right *muti* or he'll take the ox whip to him. Jesus, that did the trick. He gives my ma such a purge I didn't stand a chance. Just after the sun comes up, I come down—born on the twenty-fourth like a good little Christian who knows his place."

Paul Rampaul broke into a wide grin.

"What the hell's the joke, coolie?" Kramer snarled. "My ma's dead before the sun goes down again."

He tossed back the brandy and walked out, hating himself, astonished at himself for disclosing what, up until then, had been known only to the Widow Fourie. But this, like every other twenty-fourth of December, had been a bad, bad day.

And there was another half hour to go before midnight.

With Shabalala handcuffed to the armrest in the back of the Anglia, Zondi got it back on the road and started for home. He could not drive as fast as he wanted to, for there were no white stones to define the road's border in his headlights. But he was determined to reach the tar at least when Christmas Day began.

His prisoner had already given his reasons for being in Jabula— innocent reasons, of course. He had claimed that news of the eviction of Robert's Halt had reached him through a cousin soon after he had parted with his town wife, Lucy, the afternoon before. This had been a terrible shock to him, and he had been very anxious to help his family set up their new home. As his employer was going to be late, it had not been possible to take his leave properly. He could not write a note and, in his haste to leave and find a bus, he had not thought of asking Lucy to pass on a message. Besides, he was not sure what he was doing was within the law. It had seemed possible to get to Jabula and back without his boss knowing. But the place had been much farther away than he had thought.

So far, Zondi had made no mention of the murder.

The road began to zigzag up into the hills where the guinea fowl had met its end. If Zondi could get over them in ten minutes, he would just reach the tar in time. Then he could really open up.

"Shabalala?"

"Yes, my father?"

"If this story you tell me is true, why then did you hide in that hole? What had you to fear from me?"

"You? I do not understand."

"Look, did you think I was a GG spy, come to see what men were in Jabula?"

"I never think these things. I see you only when you are with the women."

And running before them, no doubt. Just as well for him he left that out.

"Then why did you hide, *skelm?*"

"Not *skelm,* my father!"

Zondi jerked the wheel hard over, drifting wide on a bend, then slamming on his brakes. A cry of pain came from the back seat as the American cuffs, which tightened if you tugged on them sharply, bit into Shabalala's wrists. Zondi built up speed again.

"I want no bloody lies!"

"True's God, my father, true's God. Shabalala tells you no lies."

"Then why "—Zondi jerked the wheel slightly—"why did you get in that hole—the grave?"

"Because I saw the car."

"This one?"

"No, the car that is blue."

Zondi could not help losing acceleration.

"What car do you mean?"

"It come by along the road. I see it and I am afraid."

"Why so?"

"I think my boss is very angry and he comes to take me away and punish me."

"But your boss had a white car. I've seen it."

"This is the car of his friends, my father."

"How do you mean?"

"Big men, they come and talk with my boss. They put fear in me. They are like—like . . ."

"So you thought your boss had got his friends to help look for you, right? And maybe he was with them?"

"Yes, my father. True's God."

And it sounded like it, too. But Zondi was conducting this interrogation with his back turned, and needed to see how the eyes moved. He adjusted his rear-view mirror so that it reflected the stress-gray face of Shabalala. The car's vibrations and the weak cabin light made such details as pupil size impossible to judge, yet it was a more satisfactory arrangement.

"These men in the blue car—tell me more about them. Do you know what they are called?"

"No, my father."

"What do you think their business was with your employer?"

"I only give them food, then go."

"You must have heard something."

"I cannot speak Afrikaans."

"Not understand one word? Rubbish, Shabalala! Do you want the car to dance again?"

"No, no, that is terrible! I will think."

The Anglia rattled over the ridge of hills and started down the short run to the tar road.

"Well, Shabalala?"

"Maybe they have the same work. They talk of a boss sometimes when I wash the dishes."

"And that's all? Do you know what Boss Swart's work is?"

"No, my father. He never told me."

"You like him?"

"Oh, yes, a very good man."

Just to keep Shabalala in the right frame of mind, Zondi allowed the Anglia to judder violently over corrugations around a sharp left-hander.

"In what way was he a bad man, Shabalala? Is any boss altogether a good man?"

"Boss Swart never asks me to do women's work."

"That's good, but can't you think of anything you don't like about him?"

Shabalala plainly made an effort to recall something that would please.

"He has strange ways sometimes, my father."

"Like what?"

"He sends me to fetch parcels from cars."

Zondi glanced up sharply into the mirror.

"You steal them?"

"No, no, my father! True's God I never steal. I take from the back cupboard of the car with a key."

"Where do you get this key?"

"Under the tire."

"And then?"

"I told you truth. I take the parcel, not heavy, just paper, leave the key in the lock place."

"How many times have you done this?"

"Three."

Zondi had another question half formed when it happened. A blue Volkswagen suddenly appeared from behind him, hurtling out of the night through his own dust, which, together with the unaligned rearview mirror, had kept its lights from catching his eye.

There were two men in it, white men and tough, who waved to Zondi to pull over and stop.

Shabalala gave a whimper and cringed back against the door. Zondi thought fast, drove fast, conceding not an inch of the road. Wheel to wheel, the two vehicles raced down toward the plain. Then the moon was snuffed out by black cloud, leaving the Anglia's headlights to give only a split second's warning of the next turn.

In those final seconds, Zondi decided to believe every word Shabalala had spoken. Which meant that the story of parcels was one the lieutenant must hear—and nobody was going to stop him.

So when the Volkswagen cut in, its passenger screaming abuse and its horn blaring, Zondi braked and tried to swing across its tail. He made it, caught a small boulder under his right front wheel, and felt the steering go.

He stamped on the brake. The Anglia, fit only for the scrapheap from the start, could take no more. The next pothole was enough to fracture its hydraulic system and the brake pedal sank soft to the floor.

The hand brake worked, but thin air gave the tires nothing to grip on. And there was no need at all for the brake at the bottom of the cliff.

nine

Christmas Day had more than dawned when Kramer awoke with a taste in his mouth like reindeer dung. Which would teach him to sleep on his back. As for his pillowcase, all he had in it was pillow, but it felt full of surprises—like yule logs, rocks, and old spark plugs. Hell, what a hangover. Maybe Mrs. Delmain would have an aspirin or something.

He rolled off his divan and took his clothes from their hanger behind the door, sniffing suspiciously at his shirt. It ponged, so it was definitely time for a new one; he took one out of its wrapper and put it on.

Then he tidied the room. All it had in it was the bed, the hanger, a cardboard box of personal papers, and an empty wardrobe, so it did not take long. His towel and shaving things he left in the communal bathroom, having spread it around among the other lodgers that he had a skin ailment. This concentration solely on essentials caused Mrs. Delmain considerable distress, and time and again he had had to turf out desks and other rubbish she felt he ought to have a use for. But at heart she was a good woman, and might help a sick man.

It was interesting how moods could change. Despite the headache, his own had much improved, and he quite looked forward to spending the day at the typewriter compiling an accident report that would have Colonel Muller bawling Colonel Du Plessis up the wall. As for detail,

107

he was going to have every blade of grass on Wallace's lawn numbered. But seriously, the report would be an evident and deplorable waste of a senior officer's time: that was the point to be made.

Kramer went along the passage, shaved in his customary fifteen strokes, and met Mrs. Delmain on the landing.

"Happy Christmas, Lieutenant! Smell the turkey?"

"Very nice."

"Then you'll be in for once? Please say yes."

"There's this murder," he said, watching her face turning respectful in the hope of a snippet of inside information. "Done with a cotton reel, but don't say."

"Oh, you can always trust me, Lieutenant, you know that!"

"It's too sordid, Mrs. Delmain. Sorry."

Far from being disappointed, this single piece of misinformation would keep her happy for hours over her cooking. And her sewing, come to that. She beamed gratefully at him.

"I wish you'd join us at the table this once. After all, you're never here for the meals you pay for—and it is a special occasion."

"I could eat an aspirin if you've got one."

"Headachy? Well, I'm sure I can manage something better than that. Just you go to your room and I'll bring it up."

He waited, half expecting to have the tablet served with stuffing, but was handed instead a cut-crystal glass filled with egg yoke and Worcestershire sauce.

"You're one of the best, Mrs. Delmain," he said gratefully. "I should have told you, they used the needle as well as the reel."

"Dear, dearie me!"

"I'm better already."

"Oh, I've got this message for you; my hubby took it a minute ago."

"Ta."

He read it quickly, twice, and then gave Mrs. Delmain a hug that damn near made her break wind.

The Widow Fourie and the children had their heads out of the Orange Express as it drew into Trekkersburg station. They waved. And it was all as if nothing had happened.

"Hello, Trompie."

"My girl."

"Happy Christmas, Uncle Trompie!"

"Same to you, kids. Where's the rest of your luggage?"

"It'll come later. Didn't have time to pack."

Only the children had anything to say all the way back to the flat. Kramer and the Widow Fourie had never gone much on words just for the sake of words.

When she did speak, it was to exclaim in dismay at the mildew on her leather sofa and at the other damage wrought by high temperatures and humidity in an unoccupied home.

"How's the time, Trompie?"

"Eleven."

"Want to go and see what your friends got from Father Christmas?" she asked the eldest girl.

"Let's go!" came a chorused reply.

One day the children would realize what such suggestions were all about. Kramer wondered what they would think of him then. He cared about this, quite a lot, sometimes.

Then he and the Widow Fourie made their love and got green mold in uproarious places.

To such effect that, a whole hour later, she was still sniggering as she came out of the bathroom in her old pink housecoat and announced that dinner would soon be served.

"Where from? There's no shops open. I thought maybe we could find a hotel."

"From here."

And she opened her hatbox, which had indeed seemed bloody heavy, and revealed roast turkey, pudding, and all the trimmings. A cold Christmas dinner was the kind of sanity few but the Widow Fourie were blessed with.

"I can help?"

"You can talk to me while I get it ready. How have things been down at CID? It seems months since I . . ."

She left it at that, trusting him. He honored that trust.

"*Ach*, a few decent cases till this week, then all hell broke loose. Muller's gone up to the Free State and Du Plessis is in charge."

"God, no."

"Giving old Zondi and me a bloody run for our money, I can tell you. He's on one job, me on another."

"Oh?"

Then he told her all about it, and all about the Wallace saga and the girl Samantha Simon, who had a surprise coming her way.

"But that's wrong, Trompie. You should have told her, poor thing."

"Let this be a lesson."

"You don't think she's learned enough already?"

He wandered out into the dining room, deposited the cutlery with a crash, and came back to lean on the kitchen table.

"Okay, so I'll give you her address, my girl. You tell her."

"Not my job."

"Is it mine? She's not down as next of kin."

The Widow Fourie lost patience with the turkey and wrenched off its right leg.

"Boogs I a drumstick!" Kramer said, mimicking child slang.

"Sorry," she replied. "You know they always go to the twins. The fact is, Trompie, I think you're wrong and you'd better see this Samantha."

"I've got till tomorrow."

"Don't put it off too long."

"My girl," he said, patting her on the rump.

Then the children came galloping in again and made a vain bid to snatch what goodies they could, but their mother was too quick for them.

"What were the presents like?" she asked.

"Not bad, Mum."

"I liked the doll Hettie got!"

"Little Hettie Boskop? Has she grown any bigger?"

"No!"

"Yes, she has!"

"Liar!"

"Look, kids, quieten down or I'll get Uncle Trompie to deal with you."

"It was nice when you weren't with us, Uncle Trompie."

"Yes, it was. Wasn't it, Mum? We never ever had to be quiet."

"Now who's telling fibs?"

"Why didn't you give us any presents this time, Uncle Trompie?" The Widow Fourie took the turkey through.

"Because I didn't. Against the law, Dawie, to offer enticements for special preferation."

"Hey?"

"I don't care about presents," said the eldest girl. "I just like Uncle Trompie. He's my boyfriend."

"And there you have your explanation for why we're here today," said the Widow Fourie, coming back in. "Bet you had it all wrong."

Kramer avoided her eyes, drew the children with him into the dining room, and made them all take their places. He sat himself down at the head of the table. The first time he had ever done so.

The telephone rang.

"Wrong number," the Widow Fourie called out.

It had to be. As far as her few friends were concerned, she had gone away indefinitely, probably for good. A lawyer was to see to the flat.

The ringing continued.

Kramer had given the number to nobody. The flat was one place he could never be reached.

Still the telephone rang.

"Maybe it's the caretaker," Kramer said. "Wondering what's going on. He didn't expect you back."

"*Ach*, of course," said the Widow Fourie, smiling.

"Aren't you going to answer then?"

"My hands are all sticky."

"Want me to?"

"Be a dear. He knows you're big stuff in the police, so don't go making something up."

Kramer grinned and lifted the receiver.

"Oh, please God, no!" said the Widow Fourie, unable to stop herself, when she saw what happened to that cheerful face.

She came with him down to the car, leaving the children to pull the crackers on their own. They would be served their food later.

"How is it she had your number, my girl?"

"Pardon? Oh, long ago—don't you remember?—I asked Zondi to ask her to find me a washerwoman. Before I bought the machine? I gave it to her then, just to save trouble. Must have kept it by her all this time."

"I suppose she rang CID first."

"Yes, she must have."

"But bloody hell! Why wasn't I rung at the boardinghouse this morning? I got *your* message all right! Why is all this being left to a wog woman to do?"

"Perhaps they don't know at CID yet."

"Of course they do! How else did Miriam get her information? Who told *her* about it?"

"Honestly, I can't help you find answers."

"My girl?"

"Trompie?"

"This, for nobody else. You understand?"

She squeezed his arm.

"And keep me some turkey, hey?"

He drove off, watching her in his mirror all the way to the corner, then opening the throttle right up.

The telephone call had proved one thing: Zondi was totally trustworthy, for otherwise his wife would have been told that the Widow Fourie was no longer at that number.

Being declared trustworthy was, Kramer thought grimly, small consolation to a dying man.

He had planned to start inquiries at the CID building but found, when he reached there, he was in no state to perform a dispassionate disembowelment of John Pig's Bum Scott.

So he headed out along the prison road for Peacevale Hospital and had plenty of time to make mental adjustments; he knew a way of using hot blood, like the paraffin flame in a farm fridge, to bring about an ice-cold self-control in seconds. When this was achieved, he looked about him and recorded the fact that it was a nice day and not too hot —around the eighty mark—that the shacks either side of the divided highway were pleasantly bereft of any festive nonsense, that some stupid Kaffir would lose his horse for good if he could not tether it properly.

The Chevrolet swept around the animal and covered another mile before the turnoff. The side road rose steeply up, pitching visitors suddenly into a congested forecourt beneath the hospital, and making it necessary to slow right down.

Kramer slowed down, perfectly under control. He found a parking space between some doctors' cars and got out. He lit his first cigarette of the day.

Peacevale Hospital was gigantic, larger than anything for whites in the Trekkersburg district. It had a thousand beds in its wards, hundreds more in the absurdly wide corridors, and beds on the floor under beds. He hoped he would find Zondi not too uncomfortable.

He tossed his cigarette to a beggar and went in, crossing, hands in pockets, over to the admitting section.

"May I help you, sir?" asked the Bantu clerk, giving a little tweak to his glasses.

"CID. A man Zondi. You've got him?"

"It is a very common name, sir, but I'll look."

"He's CID, too."

"Oh, you mean *Sergeant* Zondi! Why, of course, sir. I know the details off pat."

Kramer almost felt amused when the man gave another little tweak to his spectacle frame, a pathetic ploy to stress his intellectualism.

"Shoot."

"Sergeant Michael Zondi was found at approximately one o'clock this morning near Boshoffdorp by a police patrol car. His vehicle had left the road and somersaulted some twenty feet into a dry watercourse. His passenger, one Thomas Shabalala, was killed instantly through loss of blood occasioned by—"

"Stop. Tell me about the sergeant."

"His condition was critical when he was moved through to the ward, sir."

"What ward?"

"Intensive care."

That sounded all right.

"What was the matter with him?"

"Such information must be obtained from the doctor in charge, sir. It is the rule here."

"You have no personal opinion?"

The clerk loved him for this small crumb.

"It is my opinion, sir, that the person in question will shortly decease. That is why I immediately communicated by telephone with the township office at Kwela Village and had them inform Mrs. Zondi of the situation."

"Where is she? She's here?"

"Arrived by taxicab moments ago."

"But why are you doing all this and not us?"

"I truly do not know, sir. The police are here with Sergeant Zondi, but they have not referred in any way to myself."

"And you say it was your idea to ring Miriam Zondi?"

"Not a service that it is possible to extend to all those who pass through these portals, of course, but I—if I can say so, sir—have a great admiration for the police."

"Long may it last, my friend."

The clerk was still trying to decide what he should make of Kramer's parting remark when he saw him step into a lift.

The operator let Kramer out on the fourth floor with instructions to keep going left until he reached a T junction, where he should turn right. Easier said than done; the corridors were crowded with beds, trolleys, and drip stands. But finally he reached a pair of swinging doors beneath the sign INT. CARE.

Kramer pushed his way through them and looked into the duty room. There a white doctor, just a baby, was offering a cigarette to his black colleague, not much more than a piccanin himself. The movement of the extending arm was quickly converted into a clumsy gesture of welcome.

"Lieutenant Kramer, Murder Squad. Where's my boy?"

The black doctor slipped a stethoscope into his long white coat, smiled shyly, and made good his escape. Kramer stepped aside for him.

"Dr. Smith-Jenkins, Lieutenant. Pleased to meet you."

"Yes, yes, but Zondi—how is he?"

"Not too good, I'm afraid."

"The facts."

"Severe loss of blood, fractured arm, lacerations, head injury. He's in a coma."

"*Coma?* Since when?"

"Dr. Mtembu has just notified me this very minute."

"The coon who was in here?"

"Dr. Mtembu, as I said."

"I see."

What Kramer saw was red. Here was this bloody little puppy, sitting on his fat arse letting a Kaffir run errands for him instead of being there at Zondi's bedside himself, doing all he could. But he would have to be careful.

"And so, what are you going to do about it, doctor?" Kramer asked lightly.

"Me? Nothing. The sergeant is his patient."

"Not for long."

"Pardon?"

"I'm getting the District Surgeon up here. It's a police case; Dr. Strydom handles all police cases."

"But he's been already, Lieutenant. Okayed Dr. Mtembu for his neurological experience, then went down to E ward to see that constable stabbed last night."

"Jesus!"

A short word that said everything, and more, Kramer thought. Perhaps too much. This Smith-Jenks—or whatever it was—had an odd look in his eye.

"You see," said Kramer, "this boy might have had some information I wanted—he was on an important case. Makes me bloody mad that nobody tells me what's going on until it's too bloody late."

"Not necessarily, Lieutenant."

"You mean he'll live?"

"I wasn't thinking of that; no, just that a Lieutenant Scott has been with him since he was brought in."

"When was that?"

"About ten—ten-thirty."

And Kramer had been at the Hunter's Moon boardinghouse up until eleven.

"Zondi was conscious?"

"Off and on, yes."

"Thank you, doctor. Which way, please?"

"Well, actually, Lieutenant—"

"*Which bloody way, man?*"

The doctor stood up, not in indignation but in fright. Kramer's crashing fist had put a splintered dent in the plywood desk top.

"Roo—Room Ten."

"Ten?" Then, with an effort, "No hard feelings, doc."

Kramer turned and walked straight into Scott, who at that moment appeared in the doorway.

"Stick around, Tromp!"

"You!"

"Who else? Been keeping an eye on old Zondi through there—he's having a kip."

"I want words with you, Scott."

"Fine. Okay to leave us alone?"

"Be delighted," blurted Dr. Smith-Jenkins, on his way as if the President had called for an enema.

And giving Kramer just enough time to adjust once again: outwardly, he relaxed and smiled; inwardly, he brought his blood back to a point above freezing.

"I don't know about you," he said to Scott, "but these bloody quacks bloody well get on my nerves sometimes. Christ, all I did was ask how

Zondi was and he goes off with all these bloody long words."

"*Ach*, I know, Tromp. Smart alecks, that's what they are."

Scott's tone was sympathetic, but his eyes suspected something. So what.

"Can you tell me then, John? About Zondi?"

"Not much. The poor Kaffir's had a hammering. Shabalala was killed in the smash, you know. Mtembu says it'll be two days before he can say how it'll be with him."

"So now I know. Thanks, man."

"A bloody shame."

"Uhuh."

Kramer helped himself to one of the doctor's cigarettes on the desk and took a light off Scott.

"Tell me, John, exactly what happened?"

"Zondi doesn't remember."

"Uhuh."

"First we knew about it, there's this farmer up that way, near a resettlement area called Jabula, who rings his local station to say he thinks there's been a crash."

"Jabula?"

"You've got quite a clever little bugger there, Tromp, man. Seems Shabalala's lot were moved to this place two days ago and Zondi got on to it. He made his arrest at Jabula; I've got that out of him."

"Why did the farmer just *think*?"

"It appears that the car went right down this cliff and into a small gorge thing. It was dark and the bloke couldn't get down himself. He saw the car go over—or at least he thinks he saw it. You know what people are like. Anyway, he gets home and gives the locals a ring."

"Time?"

"Around midnight. Well, our lot have got a van going out to a report of a faction fight, so they stop for a look. They find the car, see it's police from the cuffs, and think everybody has kicked it. Then they notice Zondi is breathing and haul him out and send for an ambo, which brings him down here."

"Time?"

"Arrived in Peacevale about ten-thirty."

"Hell, what's with this ambulance? Did they have to pedal it?"

"Sorry; first they take Zondi to a mission hospital close by, but they haven't got proper equipment so they come on down the whole way. Get here and tell CID and the duty officer phones me at the hotel."

"You poor sod. Bet you had a headache this morning, hey?"

"I'll say. Anyway, I tell them to find you and I come up here meantime."

"Fine. You say Zondi told you he made his arrest at Jabula. Anything else?"

"*Ach,* man, he was rambling a lot, hey."

"Like?"

"Nothing I could put in my notebook. Had some idea that women were after him, hundreds of them, the randy bastard."

"And him a married man. Talking of that, they tell me downstairs that his woman, Miriam, is here, too."

"That's her name, is it? Came about twenty minutes ago and Mtembu said maybe it was right she should see him in the circumstances."

"She there now?"

"Was when I last saw."

"Uhuh."

Kramer crushed the last inch of the cigarette into a kidney bowl, yawned, and sighed.

"Oh, well," he said wearily, "I suppose I'd better have a look in at him."

"What for?"

Kramer looked at Scott blankly.

"Hell, I don't know," he replied, with a lie and a laugh. "I suppose just to see how much damage there is. Maybe I'll have to get myself a new boy."

"On the way out anyway, Tromp. I'll show you."

Kramer followed Scott back down the passage almost to the double doors and was taken into a two-bed ward.

There he allowed himself to notice only two things: the fact that

Miriam was no longer present, and that Zondi looked unnaturally small under the sheet. It was all he could take.

Then he and Scott went by lift down to the admitting hall.

"Oh, by the way, Tromp, the Colonel wants us blokes at his place for drinks at three."

"*Hey?*"

"Honest, I'm not bulling you."

"But just you and me?"

"That's what he said."

"Jesus, wonders will never cease."

"Now I'd better get back to the hotel or I'll miss my Christmas dinner. Join me?"

"No, thanks, John, but ta all the same. Let's say I've got a turkey of my own, hey?"

The food remained untouched on its plate, but the Widow Fourie did not press him. She sat opposite drinking Cape wine from a sherry glass.

"Where are the kids?"

"Out. I sent them round to Hettie's place."

"Day after tomorrow I'll get them all something."

"No need, but they'll be pleased. Very."

"I want to."

The Widow Fourie poured another glass to the brim and pushed it across.

"No, thanks, my girl."

"You think he'll die then?"

"Who knows?"

"I'm sorry for Miriam. If he does, she'll have all those little piccanins to feed."

"The twins are quite big."

"Funny she didn't stay longer at the hospital, Trompie."

"Think so? Christmas Day? Five kids?"

"Of course. You forget with them, don't you?"

"Plus the fact she was offered a lift home."

"You didn't say that before."

"Not important. Huh!"

She responded eagerly to his first sign of a lighter mood in over an hour.

"What's funny, Trompie?"

"This bastard Scott. He fixes for a van to take her back to Kwela Village but doesn't say. I got it off a wog in Admitting. What's wrong, does he think I'll say he's a Kaffir-lover?"

"You men!" She laughed hopefully.

But Kramer had relapsed into introspection. He had already accepted the fact that Bantu Detective Sergeant Michael Zondi was as good as dead, so it was not some suspect sentiment that gnawed at his guts. Gnawed like a rat, nibbled and tore with the tiny teeth of tiny details barely noticed, now forgotten. A rat called intuition, perhaps. But no, intuition was not something tangible with a tail, and a fetid smell about it. For he could swear he had more than once seen this rat out of the corner of an eye, had caught a whiff of it in passing. Of course, a mouse in the guts could feel as bad, when you came to think about it. They had little sharp teeth, too. And stank.

He stood up and reached for his jacket.

"Off to the Colonel's after all?" asked the Widow Fourie.

"Miaow," replied Kramer.

ten

Colonel Du Plessis lived with his unlovely family in a large bungalow on a small holding two miles west of Trekkersburg along the Tierkop road. There he boasted of maintaining the great agricultural traditions of his pioneer forefathers by employing three Kaffirs to grow flowers for the market. His specialty was delphiniums.

In honor of the day, however, pride of place in his lounge had been given to the top of a dead pine tree painted silver. From its branches hung chocolate dainties wrapped in gold paper.

"Take one," the Colonel encouraged Kramer. "Go on, man, we don't mind."

Kramer minded, for several reasons—among which was the fact the sodding awful things had melted in the heat.

"No, thanks, sir. Never gone for sweet things."

"*Never*, Lieutenant?"

This archly merry remark had come from the Colonel's wife, Popsie, a pinch-faced nympho who looked out on the world from between her fine legs. Alas for poor Popsie, her efforts on behalf of her spouse had finally placed her with him on a pedestal where no sane man, whatever his motive, would dare venture. Which had a moral: bitches in heat should never climb lampposts; some get stranded and miss all the fun.

She yapped on, unheeded by Kramer, as they moved out, with their drinks, to the patio and the swimming pool, where Scott was tightening the cord of a borrowed pair of trunks. Good thinking.

"Hello there, Tromp, old mate. Coming in?"

"Not today."

"Hell, it's hot enough for you, isn't it?" said the Colonel.

"Yes, sir, but I've got work to do."

"What work?"

"My report on the Wallace case. You said you wanted it—"

"*Ach*, that was yesterday, man! Things were different."

"How so, sir?"

"Well, the Swart case was still open, for a start. It had me really worried, I can tell you, specially when Sergeant Zondi didn't report back. I was all nervy last night in the hotel. Don't you remember?"

Kramer's recollection was that the Colonel had been anything but.

"Well, old son?"

"I suppose so, sir."

"See what I mean about the lieutenant, Popsie? Dedication. A hard worker—and a hard, hard man."

"Are you, Lieutenant?" she asked naughtily.

"So you're satisfied that the Swart case is complete, sir?"

"Naturally! Didn't Zondi get his man? Of course he did! Makes me ashamed I ever had a worry in my head. But of course you never doubted it for a second. Am I right?"

"Well, sir—"

"As if you would. As if you'd think twice about it. I know how long you've worked with that Bantu, Tromp, and I know you trust him. From now on, I do, too."

Kramer raised his glass and drank slowly. He needed a moment or two to catch up with this astonishing about-face on the part of one of Zondi's natural enemies. Then he realized such talk came cheap when a man lay dying.

"Even so, sir, I thought we should have more proof than a dead coon."

"You can carry things too far, Tromp! Shabalala was *handcuffed*, right? Would Zondi do that to a witness?"

"Depends on how much the witness wanted to give evidence, sir."

"Rubbish! Anyway, we have what he said to John here."

But Scott was already running along the springboard. He went up and came down like a champion, entering the water with barely a splash. Then he surfaced and churned rapidly to the far end, where he ducked under and began swimming underwater.

"Not bad," said Kramer. "Didn't know our blokes got swimming baths in the desert."

"Ha! That'll be the day, Tromp! No, he tells me that they use the one belonging to the diamond company. In there all the time; nothing else to do."

Which was a plausible answer, but not an explanation for what had actually attracted Kramer's attention: the fact that Lieutenant John Scott did not have the sort of tan, even for such pink skin, that a desert sun would give.

"But as I was saying, Tromp, our friend John in there is satisfied beyond a reasonable doubt that Zondi got our murderer for us and that's enough for me. What more can I ask?"

"Sir?"

"Weren't you listening?"

"Sorry, sir. Go on."

"*Ach*, in this heat? I've had enough. Let me put it this way: *both* cases are closed, you can forget all about them, and you can go off duty until Colonel Muller gets back. Okay?"

"But—"

"But nothing. My Christmas present to you. Take it—and that's an order!"

"And what's Zondi getting, Colonel? A Christmas Box?"

Popsie Du Plessis drew back, startled by the audacity of Kramer's words, however lightly spoken. That "Box" pun had barbs. She glanced apprehensively at her husband, but he merely closed his eyes and sighed.

"Only God can answer you that . . ." he began, found nothing to add, and finished up with his mouth in a pious pout.

Interesting. Remarkable, in fact, for the Colonel had built his reputation almost exclusively upon a terrifying lack of self-control. His normal response to a joke at his expense was bad enough. Add to this the humiliation of his wife being present, and you had the total abandon of manhood outraged. And yet, under severe test conditions, the reading was nil—the Colonel had done nothing. Correction: he had behaved with discretion, and this registered on another dial as Condition Abnormal. Kramer had suspected as much, and taken a calculated risk in verifying it. Now that he had the result of his experiment, however, he was damned if he understood its significance—except that the Colonel was up to something, and that something was so important it made restraint worthwhile.

"Another little drinkie, Lieutenant?" asked his hostess.

"What? No; no, thanks, Mrs. Du Plessis. Ta for the hospitality, and for asking me along, sir. I think I'll start my little holiday now."

"Good lad," said the Colonel, smiling. "Don't wait. I'll say good-bye to John for you."

When Kramer arrived back at the flat, all he wanted was a quiet talk with the Widow Fourie about the Colonel and his guest. But the children were rushing in and out, which made this difficult, to say the least.

"No, not there! I told you: over there, by the bread tin. What was that, Trompie?"

"The Colonel, him shutting up like that."

"Sure you're not imagining it?"

"Look, my girl, I know how to get that bastard going. Haven't I done it before, deliberately?"

"No."

"Hey?"

"I meant no to— Oh, for goodness' sake, boys! Can't you be more careful? I nearly had milk— What was that? Yes, you have, but it's a long time since Colonel Dupe was around."

"He can't have changed that much."

"Just a sec. Listen, you lot, if you can't do what I ask you properly, then I might as well—"

"Shut up!" shouted Kramer.

Everyone froze.

"Now finish your sentence," he said.

"All I was going to say was that it's very simple. You've said what a fuss you were going to make about writing up the Wallace business, and how Colonel Muller would go mad when he saw it. Maybe Du Plessis has realized what a fool you could make him look."

"And the Shabalala case?"

"Well, it does sound wrapped up, doesn't it? Have a heart, Trompie. Deep inside, Du Plessis may himself feel bad about Zondi. That's why you didn't get your reaction."

"Hmmm."

"Can we go now, please, Mum?"

"Shhh! Uncle Trompie's in charge."

"Yes, you go," he muttered and they stampeded out.

"Then there's the little matter of Scott's skin," Kramer said.

"Since when were you an expert on suntan?"

"*Ach,* I know what I saw!"

"Scott's an English name even if he says he's Afrikaner; the English have pink skins that don't go brown, don't they?"

"Maybe some."

"Then what you are— Hey, be careful with that box! Haven't I told you three times already?"

One of the boys sheepishly picked up a carton dropped in the hall and tiptoed past his mother into the kitchen. There a considerable collection of foodstuffs, toys, and clothes was piling up on all available surfaces.

"Do you mind telling me what the hell's going on?" Kramer demanded.

"I'm being practical."

"Oh, yes? Storing up for the winter?"

"In a way, yes."

He was puzzled by her evasiveness. The Widow Fourie had been jumpy ever since he got home.

"Where's it all coming from?"

"Oh, here and there—people in the other flats. People I knew before to talk to."

"They've taken pity on you?"

"Really, Trompie, that's not a very nice thing to say!"

"It's for the natives," said the eldest girl.

"For Zombie!" added the one who read all the comics.

"Or at least for Zondi's wife," said the Widow Fourie, with a self-conscious grimace. "I went round the flats and told them what had happened, how he'd caught a European's killer and had the accident. They had so much stuff, it being Christmas, it was easy to find things they didn't want. That's what the kids have been doing, collecting it up."

"Hell, what gave you this idea?"

The Widow Fourie shrugged, blinked as though her eyes were stinging.

"You forget, Trompie."

"What?"

"I know what that woman's got to go through—it happened to me once."

That came in under the belt, but Kramer had asked for it. So he shrugged, too, and went over to get his cigarettes from his jacket.

"Now I suppose I'll have to lug this lot out there?"

"Nobody's making you."

"I didn't say that."

"Mummy says we can go with you, Uncle Trompie. Can we?"

"Please let us!"

"Come on!"

"But you know they're not allowed in Kwela Village, my girl. You shouldn't have said."

"If they go with you? A policeman?"

"That's not the point. Or is the point, if you like. I can't break bylaws just to please your brood."

"Surely, Trompie . . ."

"What if we put shoe polish on, Mum? Can we go in then?"

This got a hearty laugh, and Kramer raised his hands in defeat.

There was still this gnawing in his stomach—the gnawing of not a mouse, but a rat. He knew for certain now because not an hour before he had smelled it. Picked it out of the perfumed breeze coming off the field of flowers onto the Colonel's patio.

Kramer was quite firm about one thing: the children were not to leave the car while it was in Kwela Village. They agreed to obey him implicitly.

"This is exciting, Uncle Trompie," the eldest girl said as they approached the gate to the municipal township. And she pointed to the high wire fence around it, topped with barbed wire, and to the Bantu guards with their knobkerries.

"*Ach*, rubbish," he muttered.

When the guards recognized the Chevrolet, they snapped off salutes, then almost fell over each other getting the gate swung wide open. They saluted again as the Chevrolet passed through.

"What's that, Uncle?"

"The school."

"Isn't very big."

"Ah, but you see they have school twice a day."

"I'm glad I don't go there!"

"Uncle Trompie means two different lots of piccanins have school, don't you?"

"Yes, yes. Now a bit of quiet, please."

He drove slowly down the uneven dirt surface, wary of what a careless move could do to his crankcase. He also had to count the roads going off to the left, for eight hundred identical houses made it easy to waste time going down the wrong one, and he had never seen a street sign in Kwela.

"Twenty-one, twenty-two!"

"Is this it, Uncle Trompie?"

"Look out for a path made with rusty condensed-milk tins, on your right."

The children commented on the insolence of those who idled in the path of the car. One old man deliberately walked in front of them, making Kramer brake to a standstill.

"Cheeky Kaffir," he said, hitting the horn.

His passengers took this up as a chant until rebuked for the noise they were making.

"It's just they aren't used to cars down this way," Kramer explained.

"Never, ever, Uncle Trompie?"

"Well, maybe a few taxis—and there's a bloke over there with an old crate."

"It's a 1940 Dodge," said the eldest boy, who knew about cars.

He was wrong, 1945, in fact, but Kramer had this gnawing to distract him.

"There's some tins! Over there! Look!"

And so there were. Kramer pulled the Chevrolet over to the side and cut the engine. Almost immediately Miriam Zondi came out of the house, apron held up to her mouth in both hands, and she looked at him with dread, fearing bad news.

So he jumped out with a wave, and told the children to wave, too.

"*Hau*, Boss Kramer. I was thinking—"

"Last I heard, Mickey was fast asleep and getting better every minute, Miriam. But he'll have to stay in Peacevale a few days at least, so I've just brought you a little something."

Her eyes narrowed. Christ, of course: if anything would come as a sign of Zondi's ultimate sacrifice, it was the bounty of white strangers piled in the Chev's trunk. While the little bugger's heart still beat, she was entitled to be without it.

"Boss Kramer?"

"I've got Mickey's pay."

"He left that here before he went in the car."

"Oh, did he? But I mean his Christmas bonus. Here, I borrowed some so it's not in its packet."

He handed over two one-rand notes.

Miriam took them with hardly a glance.

"Not much, but the first Christmas bonus the police ever paid," Kramer added, fairly certain the payment would remain unique—it was his own money.

"You come inside, Boss Kramer?"

"Why not? Just for a minute."

It was the other unique occasion, in its way, for although Kramer had entered hundreds of homes exactly like it, so that he knew the size of the two rooms almost down to the statutory inch, he had never been into the one rented by Zondi.

This particular house was distinguished by its consummate neatness, and the fact that Miriam, who had once been maid to a very rich lady, was not without taste. Kramer was very taken by the newspaper pattern she had scissored to fringe the shelves of her sideboard, and by the lines she had scored to simulate planking in the stamped earth floor.

"Very nice," he said, being offered the steadier of two chairs. "Mickey has a good woman. Where are the youngsters?"

"By the river."

"Very nice, too."

Miriam, who felt it proper to remain standing, curled one large toe over the other. She looked across at the Primus stove.

"The boss would like some tea?"

"Don't bother, thanks, Miriam."

"I can do it quickly."

"Fine. Yes, please."

Kramer suspected that by now the Widow Fourie's kids would have slit open his seats, and might even be trying to drive themselves away. He was mad to accept the tea, but it was not an easy thing to just walk out.

"Tell you what, Miriam," he said. "I'm just going out to the car for a minute; won't be long."

He had remembered that among the gifts to the Zondi family was a large packet of hard candies. He distributed these among his entourage, received promises of good behavior to be rewarded by a trip to the bird sanctuary, and went back to the house.

Miriam, true to her word, had a large cup waiting for him on the table. She had not poured one for herself, so he was glad to have acted as he did.

"They were kind to you this morning, I hear."

"Who, boss?"

"The officers at Peacevale—gave you a ride in a van back here."

"*Hau!*"

"What's the matter, Miriam?"

"It is nothing, boss."

"You tell me."

Her bitterness had come as a complete surprise.

"Is it kind for a woman to be told she must go, leave her husband who is dying?"

"Someone said this?"

"They said I must leave Mickey, go in the van."

"When?"

"Just after you come to the hospital, Boss Kramer. I hear your voice."

"My voice?"

"Yes, boss."

Kramer noticed that his hand, the one taking a spoonful of sweetened condensed milk from the can for his tea, was shaking. He quickly got the creamy dollop into his cup and stirred. He stirred and stirred.

"So you thought it was me who sent you away?"

"Oh, no, boss! Never!"

"Uhuh. Let's get one thing straight from the start: Mickey is not certain to die, this I know. The doctor, Mtembu, told me this."

Miriam leaned against the sideboard, her head down.

"He is an African?"

"Yes, but a good doctor. I know this also."

"He did not say the same to me."

"No?"

"He said that Mickey will die, just as surely as the ox must die when the butcher hits its head with a club."

"Jesus!"

"That is why I must speak with my husband, he says; I must speak with him because never again will I hear his words."

The cup shook all the way to Kramer's lips, frightening him more than anything he had ever experienced. But Miriam kept her eyes to the ground.

"What—what did Mickey say?"

"I had to ask if he had any message for you."

"*Me?*"

"They said he would not talk to the policemen that were there. Only a little—only that he'd caught this man in Jabula."

"Shabalala?"

"Him, that one. But why do you ask this, Boss Kramer? They wrote down the message for you."

"Who did?"

"The other lieutenant, he who sat behind the curtains by Mickey's bed."

She saw her reply in Kramer's face before he had time to make up one.

"Boss? What is the meaning of these things that are happening?"

"Sit down, Miriam. Please, I want you to. Then tell me my message once more so that I can remember it."

She sat, that wide pelvis, the joy of Zondi's life, sinking slowly down on the rickety chair so its legs creaked and stiffened at different angles. To be heavy with grief could be a very literal thing.

"I forget, boss," she whispered.

Kramer waited a little while before prompting her.

"Shabalala—did Mickey speak more of him?"

"Yes. Said that you must not blame him for the death of that man."

"You're sure he said that?"

"Shabalala just run away when his wife is taken to a new place."

Kramer fought the cup back into its saucer, using every muscle of his arm to keep the bloody thing from wobbling. It clattered home. Then he stood up.

"What else, Miriam?"

She was weeping, pressing her eyes into the crook of her arm and rocking back and forward. He stretched out a hand to steady her, whipping it back just in time.

"Hey, wife of Zondi! Is this how you would be seen? Would he not be ashamed?"

That put a stop to her nonsense. Miriam looked up, proud, defiant of Fate—as Zondi had so often said, a true Zulu, a warrior's woman.

"My man said nothing else, Boss Kramer, for although he is very sick, his ears are those of a cat. He hears the men behind the curtain—I see his eyes go to them and back to me. He says he must sleep."

"And then?"

"This man Mtembu comes in and gives him a big injection in the arm. I ask why they do this, and they say my husband wishes to sleep; it will help him."

Kramer backed to the door, bringing his finger up to beat out a warning.

"Miriam Zondi, you promise that you will not say that you ever spoke to me on these matters. Understand?"

"You do not know of them?"

"Swear, woman! Mickey's life . . ."

But Kramer had not really the time to spare for melodrama. He walked from the house without another word, started the Chevrolet, and drove carefully to the gates. Then gave the Widow Fourie's children the most exhilarating ride of their lives back to the flat, where he dumped them, without ceremony, and still less explanation.

Their mother, waiting anxiously on the pavement, had to go without one, too.

eleven

G one were the abstractions, the distractions, and the self-indulgences of seemingly purposeless existence; and with them the imaginary rats, the gory brothels, the impaled effigies in wax. Lingering was an impression that the iron had entered into Kramer's soul, if such it was, to make of him a machine, resolute and ruthless. Then this idle fancy, too, was gone.

For now Kramer had a purpose and no need for anything else. A very simple purpose, suggested to him in simple words by a simple woman, and that was to solve the riddle of Hugo Swart's death by whatever method he chose. To solve it and then to wreak vengeance. As simple as that.

And he did not pause to reflect upon the possible personal consequences, any more than a man would hesitate before galloping to his fallen brother in battle.

He switched cars at Hunter's Moon and headed in the twilight for Peacevale Hospital.

Mrs. Delmain had run out to the Ford as he was unlocking it, carrying in her hand a note telling him to ring CID with reference to his Bantu sergeant, who had been hurt in an accident. Mrs. Delmain had said she took the message just as they were sitting down to the dinner he would have so enjoyed. Mrs. Delmain was a truthful woman, and a talkative one: she went on to say that the policeman on the other end had complained at having been unable to get through earlier. She knew of nobody in her establishment who had hogged the telephone that morning. Kramer thanked her kindly.

The horse he had seen earlier in the day, wandering on the Peacevale road, was dead. Broken and bundled into the ditch by a bus that had seized up a mile farther on because of a damaged radiator.

Then, against the sunset, the hospital rose in silhouette. He drove under its shadow and on, keeping an alert eye for the back road used by refuse trucks and other medically unfit traffic. He found it and circled around through the veld, closing in along a builder's track that ran among weeds to the recently completed block for nonwhite physicians. There, beside a site hut, he left the Ford and proceeded on foot.

The residence was pink brick with iron-framed windows and three floors. It had no kitchen, as presumably everyone ate over in the hospital canteen, and this eliminated one means of entry—but there was a fire escape. Kramer was moving toward it, close to the back wall, when he heard a voice unmistakably that of Dr. Mtembu. It came from a ground-floor window he had just ducked under.

"No, I am quite well," Mtembu was saying. "It is just I wish to remain in my room to study tonight."

"Then I'll give the girls your love, all right?"

"Please do," Mtembu replied, wearily, and a door closed on a laugh.

Kramer edged back. Mtembu must have just entered the room himself, for the light was still out and he was hanging his white coat on a hook in the wall. The doctor did not hear the window opening to admit an unexpected visitor. He just thumbed the switch and turned around very naturally, like a man relieved to be alone at last, not thinking at all.

His head jerked in fright.

"No noise," warned Kramer. "You were going to work, so sit at your desk."

It was a table really, but covered with heavy books and clinical notes. Mtembu sat, his hands automatically clearing a space, finding a ball pen.

"Am I to have no peace?" he said finally, peevishly, as their eyes broke contact.

"None."

"It was not what you promised."

"I promised nothing."

"Your brother officers did."

"And what was that?"

"No further impositions."

Kramer was not used to having a wog address him in such a tone, still less to hearing one speak proper English and with an English accent, too. The sheer novelty won him over.

"But do you know who I am?"

"A policeman. A lieutenant, you said."

"And my job?"

The doctor hunched his shoulders.

"I'll tell you then. My job is to see that others do their jobs properly. Only without them knowing."

A wry smile greeted this improvisation.

"You want to say something?"

"Quis custodiet ipsos custodes?"

"Hey? What bloody language is that?"

Mtembu tapped the textbook before him.

"Latin, sir. A necessary prerequisite of any student of medicine, or so those who set the syllabus would have us primitive peoples believe. Such stresses are behind me now, of course, but I must confess to a liking for the literature. The methods of warfare, the short sword and shield, have much in common with those employed by the Zulu Caesar, Skaka: the stabbing spear and—"

"Hold it! I didn't ask you for a bloody lecture, I asked what you said! Trying to swear at me, were you? Piss what?"

"Quis, sir. The quotation means 'Who shall guard the guard?' "

"Oh, yes? Well, let's say you catch on quickly, Mtembu. I like that."

"Lieutenant?" Mtembu murmured, uncomfortable.

"You're not overdoing this stuff you're giving Zondi then, Mtembu? The man is useful to me."

"I have prescribed no more than the minimal dosage, sir. It will keep him unconscious for an unlimited period without ill effect, provided care is taken with intravenous feeding."

"And his injuries?"

"To hear the circumstances of his mishap, they are mercifully slight. The arm should already have begun to knit together."

"His head injury, I mean."

"Just a bump on the back, a cut cheek—all very minor."

Mtembu had looked surprised by the question but, no doubt used to the ignorance of laymen, spelled it all out. Quite unaware he was giving Kramer his first proper idea of the situation.

"Fine. Then carry on as you are."

"I took the Hippocratic Oath, Lieutenant!" protested Mtembu in sudden rebellion.

"Then see you don't end up in court taking another one, my friend."

"Sir?"

"I guard the guard," Kramer replied. "Before you mention our little chat to anyone, and especially to a policeman, remember there is also a guard who guards *me*."

That took care of Zondi, in more ways than one. Now Kramer could concentrate exclusively on Swart. Naturally it had been a temptation to question Mtembu further, to discover how Strydom had been hoodwinked, to learn what pressures had forced the poor black sod into playing along, but unwise. Unwise because to know could have made him angry. Unwise because Kramer had within him a latent fury that needed only a single spark of emotion to set it off—to blast the buggery out of all and everything. To remain effective, he had to remain dull, plodding, bound to a logical process. And anyway, he was confident that having picked up the trail in Skaapvlei, he would ultimately be led back to Peacevale Hospital and to all the answers he could stomach.

He parked his Ford half a block from Swart's bungalow and found a footpath that ran around the edge of the racecourse behind it. Within five minutes he had stolen across the back garden, tinkered with the kitchen window, and let himself in.

This was where the game began. But first, as in all such games, he had to throw a six.

Huh, the vodka. But that had been an easy one. He was after real evidence now, and in the wake of the enigmatic John Scott, who had presumably removed everything of obvious significance. Still, if Swart had used the fridge for his booze cache, it stood to reason he might have used it for other things.

Kramer opened the refrigerator door, almost starting back as the light came on. He depressed the trip switch and ran the beam of his penlight over the shelves. Fruit, milk, eggs, a small turkey, a pudding with a plate over it, a couple of eggplants—nothing. He glanced at the freezer compartment—nothing.

Next Kramer examined the room as a whole, looking under the paper lining in each drawer, and digging a hand into the canisters of rice and sugar, well aware Swart was hardly likely to leave anything of importance where a servant might find it, but determined to overlook not a single crevice. This finally brought him to his knees and a minute examination of the floor. The linoleum, which smelled, not unpleasantly, of disinfectant, was so brightly patterned in mock mosaic that his eyes danced in their effort to spot the unconsidered trifle. So he swept a hand lightly over the surface, finding, with his fingertips, a shallow, irregular depression. He identified it as the mark made by the hearing aid when somebody, very likely the killer, had stamped on it. Kramer's hand brushed a small object a few inches to the right of the dent, up against the sink cupboard: it was some sort of electrical component, a rod half the length of a matchstick with hair-thin wire bound neatly around it and two fine silver wires at either end. It also had two yellow bands. Big deal. Scott had not been very careful with his exhibits.

Finally he was sure the kitchen had nothing to reveal, and so he began on the rest of the house. He did this with such painstaking thoroughness that his batteries gave out at one o'clock on Boxing Day morning. He moved to the study window. All Skaapvlei lay silent, all the little rabbits snuggled deep in their burrows of blankets, all with little distended bellies, brimming and bubbling with rich things, going through hell. Which was why he dared not switch on a light lest some bunny, on its way to the boggywoggy to do its business, noticed the gleam and called the cops. Which was bloody frustrating, as he had come across some papers in the desk that interested him.

Kramer realized then that he was tiring, for all he had to do was light a match. Or better still, one of the small candles stuck in that holy object in the hall. He took a candle down to the far end of the main passage, where its faint light would never be seen from outside.

First he examined brochures from two car-hire firms in Trekkersburg, both of which featured the latest models and had to be recent issues. He had come across them in the collection of motoring documents that Swart kept in his desk. They had attracted his attention because Swart's car itself was a very recent model, and he could not see why the man had been interested in renting. Unless, of course, it was for someone else.

But checking through the bank statements, he found that on four occasions Swart had himself paid by check for the hire of vehicles from a firm known as Trekkersburg Travel and Self-Drive.

Then he cross-checked the dates on the invoices from the garage where Swart had his own car serviced: it appeared from these that on four occasions, and for reasons certainly best known to himself, Swart had arranged to have two cars at the same time.

This, the first real indication that there was more to the case—in its own right—than met the eye, gave Kramer fresh impetus.

He hurriedly sorted through the other motoring papers, but was unable to find anything from Trekkersburg Travel. A little elementary arithmetic, however, based on the amounts Swart had paid, and on the charges given in the brochure, sweetened the discovery by deepening the mystery: Swart had not used his hired vehicles, on any of the four occasions, to travel farther than the first twenty kilometers that were covered in the basic tariff. Trekkersburg Travel must have treasured his custom.

What a balm to Kramer's bruises. But, in the way of all ointments, it seduced a fly. This fly buzzed a warning that Scott would have to be an idiot to miss such intriguing transactions. For a moment Kramer felt duped, then he reasoned that he had himself missed out on them first time around. It all depended on just how intent you were on finding something. Scott, about whom he was forming several theories, all kept rigorously unexamined for the sake of objectivity, had seemed to lack motivation all along.

Odd, but beside the point, for the moment.

The CID building was quiet the way it was quiet perhaps only once a year. Christmas Eve it had echoed to the indignant cries of last-minute shoplifters, assault suspects waving mistletoe, and a store Santa found with aftershave in his sack. Christmas morning it was the turn of the Housebreaking Squad, trying to placate party-goers who had party-gone without securing their homes properly. By Christmas night everybody given to criminal irresponsibility had drunk too much to exercise it. Come Boxing Day, it was quiet.

Kramer got the gist of this from grizzled Detective Constable Lourens, who, having failed his sergeant's examination for three decades, haunted the building incessantly in the hope of being there, all alone, when *it* happened—it being, apparently, something unimaginable which would make a merit promotion imperative.

"But what are you doing here at this time, if I can ask, Lieutenant?"

"*Ach*, just come to pick up a few things before I blast off for the Free State."

"Leave, sir?"

"Couple of days off. Anybody around?"

"No, sir. Duty man in Housebreaking is investigating a report in Greenside, and then there's me. Colonel was in earlier, round ten, with the new officer."

"Uhuh?"

"Made a few phone calls and went off again. From the sound of it, the Colonel was having him back to his place."

"Hmmm."

"Know what you mean, sir. Colonel Muller's my man."

Kramer gave him a wink and then began up the stairs, pausing on the landing to light a cigarette and take a look at Lourens from behind his cupped hands. It was all right: the man was back sitting in his chair in the office by the entrance, where he had put his feet in a desk drawer and dropped his chin to his chest for another of those life-sustaining catnaps.

Not that Kramer was planning to do anything illegal exactly, but he was decidedly anxious to be left to his own devices.

He had to think his way into this one, just as he always did, by a careful examination of the murder scene. His real chance had been missed in a blasé exhibition mainly for Strydom's benefit; now he had to settle for photographs, but they were better than nothing.

Scott had been given a desk in the clerk's office adjoining that used by Colonel Du Plessis. The photographs were in a brown envelope on the blotter.

Kramer shook them out and studied each of the prints very carefully, struck as always by how much more depressing things looked in mono-chrome. He turned them this way and that, wondering why they seemed unusual; it was not so much the images but the *feel* of them. Then an idea occurred to him; he picked up the clerk's ruler and measured the longest side of the photograph in his hand. There was no white margin —Photographic always printed edge-to-edge—and from one corner to the other it was nine inches. And yet Prinsloo, the resident cameraman, always spoke of "ten-by-eights."

He slipped them back in the right order into the envelope, replaced it in precisely its original position, and then went down the corridor and through Fingerprints to where Prinsloo had his domain. There he started on the negative file, finding the packet he sought almost immedi-ately. The death of Hugo Swart had been recorded on 120 film by a camera that took square pictures. Usually this meant part of each picture was lost in the enlargement, but from the top and bottom and not the sides.

The darkroom had been left in a state of readiness, with fresh devel-oper in the tray, covered by a sheet of glass, and fixer ready-mixed in a Winchester bottle. Kramer, who had learned enough of the art in a special course at police college, set to work without wasting a moment.

He selected a negative that seemed to be the same general shot which topped the pile on Scott's desk, and placed it in the enlarger's holder —having peered at it first in the light from the lamp housing but found the detail too small for the naked eye. He took a sheet of paper from the box by the easel and then racked the enlarger up so that the image it threw went edge to edge. There, on the right, was a small rectangular object about half an inch inside the full picture.

Of course, the bloody hearing aid—a mere detail. All that effort wasted. Yet, talking of effort, someone had gone to the trouble of trimming all the prints down to an odd size. Perhaps he should make a print in case there was something else that had escaped him in the reversal of tones.

So Kramer flipped on the red filter, replaced the ten-by-eight with an unexposed sheet, gave it a burn for five seconds, then dumped it in the first tray. He tipped a little of the fixer into the next one along, did a taste test on the acidity of the stop bath, and came back to watch.

In the yellow light of the safety lamp, faint shadows stole onto the white bromide, darkening into two dark dots and an irregular streak; they were the eye sockets of Hugo Swart and his spilled blood. Shade by shade, the picture built up: the dead man's face rounded then slackened, the pieces of glass sharpened to bright splinters, a stain appeared on the trousers by the crotch that had not been noticeable before. Finally each tiny particle of silver, which in other circumstances might have merged with others to create a thing of beauty, proclaimed the basic ugliness of man and his works.

And there seemed nothing remarkable about the hearing aid whatsoever.

Kramer pitched the print into the stop bath and then into the fixer. He lit another cigarette from the one burned down in the ashtray, and then snapped on the white overhead light. When he looked this time, it was not with any hope of seeing anything significant.

But he did. He saw very faint parallel gray lines, too pale for visibility under the yellow safety, and rendered almost indistinguishable by the disruption of grain, running round and round the hearing aid.

God, what an oversight! When the priest had remarked upon the fact that the gadget had suffered willful damage, Kramer's reaction had been one of professional intolerance. He had been annoyed that anyone who claimed to know his fellow men would not also know that the more violent of them often took out excess feelings on inanimate objects associated with their victims—just as a kid might thump his sister, then kick down her pile of blocks. He had wanted to tell him how burglars crap on beds and pee into dressing tables. He had got caught up with a trifle and quite missed the appallingly obvious.

Which went something like this: The assumption had been that the hearing aid fell to the floor during the death struggle. But here it was, its lead wound neatly around it, as it would be when the fastidious Swart was not wearing it. And yet the priest had stated the radio was on when he found the body—which was a lot of use to a deaf man.

"Hold it," said Kramer to himself, trying to think of reasonable explanations for this gross contradiction of fact. There was the thought that the killer had switched the radio on to smother the sound of his retreat; but this was rubbish, because if he had been quiet enough to take Swart by surprise— Wait a minute. That presupposed Swart *could* hear, and turned the argument on its head.

Kramer started again. A deaf man comes into his kitchen and switches on the radio. It is about nine o'clock so probably he wants to hear the news. Then he decides to unhitch his aid—probably bothersome in the heat—and does so. This cancels the radio for him anyway, and perhaps he is about to switch it off when the killer attacks.

And yet he was expecting a visitor at any minute, the priest had arranged to call, he would want to hear the knock. All right, so the priest had been early by ten minutes, but nobody relied on callers to time their arrivals so exactly.

The counter to that was simply that Swart had intended to go and wait out on the front veranda for the priest, but was struck down before he could do so.

The counter-counter was that this left him very little time to enjoy his illicit drink, which he would hardly carry out with him. Or again, he might, seeing it was vodka.

Counter, counter, counter. But when you came right down to it, a hearing aid was like a heavy-framed pair of spectacles: habitual users were unlikely to be aware of their weight and inconvenience any more than a well-stacked dolly was aware of her mams. Unless, of course, in each case their equipment was sham. Then, in the privacy of the home, during a heat wave, shedding could well take place, foam rubber the lot.

—"Man, oh, man . . ."

Kramer lifted the print out of the fixer, swished it through the wash, and then rolled it flat on the small glazer. While it dried, he tidied up the bench and left nothing for Prinsloo to find out of place.

Then he went back to the clerk's office and compared the two pictures. He had chosen exactly the same negative—there was a water mark in the same place on each one—and the degree of enlargement had been, within a millimeter, identical. Which suggested Prinsloo had done as he had done—blown it up to fit the paper and pressed the button. It also suggested that somebody had trimmed off the hearing aid from the one picture in which it appeared, and then had cut the other prints down to give them a uniform size.

Without actually handling them, Kramer might never have noticed any difference; it was also extremely unlikely that the examining magistrate would have given the dimensions a thought. It was just the echo of Prinsloo's "ten-by-eights" that had triggered him off. And was, in the final analysis, the crux of the matter.

Suspicion bred suspicion, Kramer knew that, but felt the hearing aid itself now warranted his attention.

But before going along to the exhibits room, he made a quick check on Lourens. The friendly ghost was still snuffling and snoring away. The ball pen lay where Kramer had left it on the duty book after signing in. Good.

He used his own key to open the heavy door and locked it again behind him. Then he began a hunt along the shelves, prodding and peering and pulling at labeled plastic bags half hidden by larger items, such as an enigmatic chamber pot. His heartbeat stepped up as he reached the end of the last shelf empty-handed. The sodding thing was not there.

Wait a minute, though. He had just remembered that the Chevrolet had been clean out of plastic bags; Zondi just may have used a few of the old issue of paper ones that had been lying around in the glove compartment, and there were a couple of them back near the door which he had taken to date from old unsolved cases.

The first paper bag had Zondi's careful printing on the outside and inside it were the fragments of a broken glass. And the other contained a hearing aid, again identified in Zondi's hand. Kramer shook the bag and heard pieces of innard rattle about. That was as far as he could go, knowing bugger all about electronics, but there was a bloke on his private list of experts who could tell soon enough if there was anything significant in the way that picture had been trimmed.

twelve

Bob Perkins was away over Christmas. Kramer hid the accumulation of milk bottles behind an azalea bush, spat at the cat very realistically, slammed the garden gate behind him, and stalked to his car. Bloody hell, Bob had been perfect for the job; he had worked on a burned tape Zondi found in the Le Roux case and come up trumps. He was also, being a yoga fanatic and teetotaler, the sort of bloke you could rouse at four on a public morning-after and expect to deliver a sensible opinion—even if his funny little woman pupped in the pantry in protest. But Bob was away over Christmas and that was that. Except Kramer still had to find himself another whiz kid who would *(a)* know what he was talking about; and *(b)* not mind talking about it before breakfast. Patience was, in Kramer's view, a vice, particularly when he had to return the hearing aid before anyone noticed it was missing.

He forked left past the hospital, catching sight of a nurse at a high window. He slowed down. She was sneaking her last cup of coffee at the end of a long night shift, probably finding the new day as unreal as he did, probably praying the ambulance men would not be delivering before seven. She raised her cup to him, laughed, and backed away. Any girl, especially in a nurse's uniform, looked beautiful at that distance, even desirable. That she was perhaps as plain as a pancake just made the brief encounter all the more poignant.

He wondered if the Widow Fourie was awake yet or, indeed, if she had slept at all; his sudden departure on Christmas Day might have set her thinking those thoughts again. He wondered if Miriam Zondi was asleep, or still twisting knots in her handkerchief. He had no doubt that Zondi himself was asleep.

Kramer's train of thought meandered about and stopped at every siding, but finally it brought him to where he should have driven in the first place: Trekkersburg Fire Station. It had traveled by way of ambulance men, who were also firemen, who had a radio link-up between their vehicles, who relied on Leading Fireman Ralph Brighton to keep this equipment in perfect order, who was a transistorized nut case. A genius.

He braked on the concrete apron outside the high, wide doors and brought the Ford right up to the watch room door. The duty fireman left his switchboard and leaned across the counter.

"What's up, cock?" he called out.

Tommy Styles, like Brighton, was another honest-to-Gawd Englishman, who had gone through the Blitz then got the hell out of a country with old buildings.

"Kramer, cock."

"Oh, aye?"

The Ford door clicked shut and Kramer took the three steps in a stride. Styles opened the counter flap.

"Sun fair blinded me. Don't say you've gone and set fire to some poor bleeder this time—dead nasty, the stories I hear."

His attitude toward the law was typical of the station's limeys: unusual to say the least, at times—incredible as it seemed—almost disrespectful. Not that it mattered; just something in their upbringing.

"Where's Brighton?"

"His flat. Only got in at half three."

"On ambulance?"

"Native maternity. Had to wash his ambo out, too, when he got back —hasn't got the touch, y'know. Won't be happy if he's wanted before his tour ends."

Now this was something else about firemen, as a whole this time, which Kramer found perplexing: they did all their own chores. The only wog employed on the premises was an old *keshla* who handed wrenches to the mechanic. The fire chief had once muttered something about discipline, which was patently absurd; as anyone trying the same trick down at the charge office would soon find out. Hey ho, he had begun to wander.

"Sorry, but I want to see him. This minute."

"On your head be it!"

Styles crabbed along the communications panel in his special chair, walked his fingers up a row of buttons, and pressed the second from the top.

"No phone?"

"Said you wanted him chop-chop. This should see to that nicely."

The huge clock above them tapped fifty seconds off the year and then down a shiny brass pole, in time-honored fashion, came Leading Fireman Brighton. Kramer, looking through the glass partition into the fire engine hall, saw him absorb the jar of his landing with a neat bend of the knees, do up the last button of his long white coat without pausing, and come cursing through into the watch room. He reached under the counter, where there were two piles of folded blankets, and snatched out one fluffy and one worn.

"Come on," he said. "Which? European or native? And where's me bloody mate?"

"Morning, Brighton. Like a word."

"Lieut! You bastard!"

"In your room?"

"And you're a right bugger, Tommy! Got my youngest squawking his ruddy head off, you have! Wait till I tell the missus; she'll have your—"

"Wot? Me with a police escort and all?"

"Look," said Kramer softly, "just watch it."

Good; they had lived in the Republic long enough to appreciate what that meant. Both men went slightly red and Styles took the blankets away to replace them. Brighton waved a hand at the staircase.

Kramer went ahead until the second landing, where he stepped aside to allow Brighton to unlock the door to the radio workshop. It was so cluttered with loudspeakers, wire, electric cord, circuit boards, jagged metal sheeting, valves, things with knobs, and other junk, the untidy bugger had to kick aside quite a bit before there was room enough inside for two.

"Close the door and lock it."

Brighton raised an eyebrow briefly but followed orders.

"Something I've done?"

"Something you're going to do."

"Oh?"

"If you will, please, man."

"Couldn't wait?"

"No."

"To do with what, though?"

"All this," answered Kramer, waving vaguely about him. "I've got a little problem just up your street. Our radio bloke is off for Christmas."

Again the quick arch of an eyebrow.

"Besides, this is a very confidential matter."

"Let's hear it then, Lieutenant. Take a pew."

Kramer perched on a section of worktable specially cleared for him.

"Because I don't want a word of this repeated outside these four walls, I'm going to give it to you straight—and you're going to keep your mouth shut."

"As I said, let's hear it."

"As you know, I'm Murder Squad, but right now I'm conducting a departmental inquiry. I have reason to believe that evidence has been interfered with. This evidence."

Kramer handed Brighton the paper bag, then slid off the table to give him somewhere to examine it. Brighton lifted out the hearing aid very carefully and put it down on a clean sheet of newspaper.

"Cor, what happened to this lot then?"

"Somebody smashed it with their heel."

"I'll say."

Brighton bent over the hearing aid and tutted and grumbled worse than Strydom over a mangled toddler.

"Where was it found, Lieut?"

"Here, see for yourself."

A man who lived his life to the tune of a wailing siren was not easily distracted by something as everyday as a corpse; Brighton hardly looked at Swart before taking his jeweler's glass to the section showing the hearing aid.

"You see," said Kramer, "another photograph to be offered in court as an exhibit has had that part of it cut away—no hearing aid showing, in other words."

"And what's your query?"

"I want to know what, if anything, there is unusual about this gadget."

"I follow."

Brighton switched his attention back to the hearing aid, picking it up and turning it around. He used his glass to examine the name *H. Swart* scratched on the back with something sharp, and rubbed a thumb on a grayish deposit.

"Any idea what this stuff is?"

"Fingerprints did that."

"Name's not been on long—no dirt yet in the marks. Easy to get off sweaty hands, too."

Then Brighton used a small screwdriver to poke about inside the instrument.

"Perfectly straightforward, Lieut; few bits missing, that's all."

"There's others in the bag."

"Heck! Take a gander at this!"

Kramer understood what had crossed Brighton's mind at almost the same instant. His hands moved forward on reflex to snatch the thing away and try it himself. But Brighton was already winding the lead to the earplug around the casing. It made four turns.

"This a trick you're playing on me?" Brighton asked suspiciously.

"Hell, no!"

"Then it isn't the same bloody hearing aid, is it?"

And he pushed across the ten-by-eight print, pointing to the broad band, which had about four times as many turns in it.

"See, the lead goes in here, molded fitting, and solders on there. This is as from factory; nobody has changed it."

"Jesus . . ."

"And that bugger in the pic's got a lead on it about three feet long. What are you after, a deaf giraffe?"

Kramer could not reply, mainly because he could hardly think straight. His cigarettes came out automatically and they lit up.

"The aids have been switched?"

"Positive of it. Does that help?"

"Man, you're doing a great job."

"Done it, as far as I can see."

"But why such a long lead? There must be a reason!"

"You'd think so, wouldn't you, Lieut? They don't make them like that. Was it his?"

"Yes, that's Swart."

"And what's he when he's at home?"

"Draftsman, worked for the province, but lived in the wrong place."

"More to it then?"

"Still waters. You get my meaning? Our friend here was mixed up in something bloody peculiar—could have been anything, but I haven't got round to that yet."

"Disciplinary, you said, Lieut?"

Brighton was shrewd, there were no two ways around that. But Kramer was quite satisfied the man was also completely trustworthy. He had that air about him.

"Yes, could be one of my officers is involved."

"That's bad."

"Very."

"But doesn't give us our answer, does it?"

"That long lead, Mr. Brighton—wouldn't it have been noticeable?"

"Wrapped around the thing in the pocket? I wouldn't say so."

"Uhuh."

They stood and stared down at the substituted hearing aid, mulling over their thoughts. Brighton tipped up the paper bag and several small electronic parts dropped out. He lifted the bag and held it against the glare coming in off the high, white-walled practice tower outside in the yard.

"Oi, oi," he said, spotting a small dark shadow in one of the glued folds at the bottom. He reached in and tried to pick out something with thick finger and thumb.

"Mind if I tear this, Lieut? Bit gone astray."

"Don't, if you can help it."

"Okay."

Brighton picked up a toffee tin filled with clutter and jiggled it about. He found an old pair of eyebrow tweezers and tried them. Out of the bag came a small brown rod, with two bands of hair-thin wire wound around it, and a silver wire sticking out either end.

"All that trouble for something that doesn't belong."

"What do you mean, man? I found one just like it on the kitchen floor, right by where the original thing was smashed. Just like that one —only the lines were yellow, not red."

"That's interesting."

"Anyway, my sergeant wouldn't put anything in the bag that didn't belong."

"He's the one you're after, Lieut?"

"Jesus, no. But he's the bloke who wrote on the bag."

"So the bag is the same one?"

Kramer took the point. The original hearing aid, and all its pieces, had been put in the bag by Zondi. Later the aids had been switched—but somebody had not taken as much trouble as Brighton to make sure everything had first been removed. Somebody who probably made the switch in the exhibits room, where the light was poor and the rod so wedged it did not rattle.

"Yes, the bag is the same bag my sergeant used. We can take it this thing belonged to the other aid; that's why it doesn't belong to this one."

"No, Lieut, it just couldn't."

"And why not?"

"Because this little beauty is a *radio* part and so, from the sound of it, was the one you yourself found."

"But his wireless wasn't touched, man."

"The one in the picture? Not surprised—you don't go putting gear like this into ruddy steam engines! Very rare, these are, and very expensive—sophisticated's what the write-ups call them. Specialized."

"In which way?"

"VHF."

"*Ach,* commercial stations?"

"Hell! Crystal set's practically all you'd need for that. No, a specialized receiver of some kind, VHF, miniaturized."

Kramer extinguished his own cigarette very carefully, rubbing it until the tobacco shredded from the paper. Sophisticated, specialized, miniaturized, and totally bewildering.

"And so?"

"Looks like we've got another problem to sort out."

"I'll be making this worth your while," Kramer said.

Brighton sat down on a loudspeaker case, fidgeted and fretted like a man trying to dislodge an idea from a corner of his mind.

"Oh, aye, but you can't give me back my kip, Lieutenant. I'm bushed, shagged; almost done my twenty-four when you buzzed. Too bloody tired. To think, I mean."

In fact, Brighton's obvious fatigue had been worrying Kramer from the outset. Now that the fireman had admitted to it, the end of their fruitful little discussion was very near at hand. Kramer just had to push him on to make one last effort.

But before he could do that, the bells went down.

"Christ," said Brighton, fully alert in a split second. "Something big's happened. I've got to scramble."

He was out of that room before Kramer could move.

The Widow Fourie was not at home. Having managed to replace the paper bag in the exhibits room without waking Lourens, and having almost bumped into Scott coming out of the communications room, Kramer had driven straight to her flat. There was a note waiting, though.

"To Whom It May Concern," it read. "Don't worry, it's just that the kids wanted to swim before the mobs arrived. See you."

So he let himself in with his own key and took a bath. He ate a leftover or two.

Then he put through a call to the fire station and learned from the duty man—Styles had gone off—that a bus up near Ladysmith had hurtled off the approach to a bridge into a dry riverbed. At least ten had died and injuries were very serious; the driver had escaped with cut hands and shock. Lead Fireman Brighton's message said he was bringing the brain damages down to Trekkersburg the minute the doctors gave the go-ahead. That could be anytime. An hour, two hours—it all depended.

"To Whom It Does Concern," wrote Kramer. "Had a bath. Had some turkey. Had to go. Things are very bad." Then he paused, trying not to add what first came to mind. Finally he wrote instead: "High Noon." And crossed it out.

But left the note with nothing torn off it and returned to the fire station.

"Brighton's been held up, sir," the duty fireman, an Afrikaner, no less, said as he entered the watch room.

"How long now?"

"If all the ambos weren't out, he'd have been relieved by now. You can ask the chief if you like."

"Won't make any difference."

"Nothing I can do for you, sir?"

"No. Got someplace I can wait?"

"Up the stairs, standby room."

"Uhuh."

"There's billiards, too, sir, if you prefer."

Kramer scowled at the thick-headed bugger and went on up to the standby room, finding two beds in it made up with blankets. He stripped one of them, loosened his tie and laces, and stretched out. Perhaps it would be as well. He slept.

A cup of coffee and a bacon sandwich woke him, furious, as the sun was setting a cheap orange against the far wall. Their breakfast aroma convinced him he had gone once around the clock.

"Take it easy," sighed Brighton, flopping onto the other bed and easing off his boots—they and his white coat had both been stained by blood. "I've had a sodding day of it."

"Hey? How long?"

"Never know your luck, do you? Drove like buggery all the way down, and what happens? I end up with four DOAs. Four! The fresh-meat express. Little kiddie and all. Should have seen the hospital—like a bleeding bomb hit it. Any road up, idea came to me around Lion's River. Could've killed meself, honest."

"What idea?"

Kramer swung around into a sitting position.

"Four, and my oppo near to blubbing in the back. Could've killed meself."

"Brighton! Take a pull at yourself, man!"

"Where my job ends and yours begins, isn't it, Lieut? When they've snuffed it. Oh, yes, I'm sorry. Trannies, you see, lots of them had trannies."

"What's that?"

"Y'know, transistor radios. On the bus. Plugged into their earholes when she went arse over tip. Started me thinking. Coils in an aid case. Radio. Need a proper aerial really, something a bit more than you'd get in a tranny. Too directional, they are. Depends on meters, wave band, all that. Around three foot should work nicely. That's where he had it, you see, aerial twisted up the lead to the ear—could fix it so it's hardly a thing you'd notice. This Swart was hooked into a receiver."

"Of what? Don't be stupid, for God's sake."

"Ah, but what was it you said, Lieut? He could've been up to *anything*? How does bugging suit you?"

"Never!"

"Can't see it any other way. Always been deaf, has he?"

Now Kramer was on his feet. He dragged Brighton up so he leaned against the headboard, and shook him until he opened his eyes again. Yes, it was the priest, Father Lawrence, who had said it: afflicted in the prime of life.

"No, no, he hasn't. Fairly recent."

154

"There you are then. I'll have your coffee if it's going."

The cup was thrust into his hands.

"How did you work that out?"

"Listen, Lieut, simple. Our lad here wants to do a bit of eavesdropping. Bit of the old fly on the wall. All right? So he puts in a bug transmitting on VHF, special frequency, short range. Now he wants to hear it but, wherever this place is, there's people who'd notice if he plugged in a receiver. Ask questions. Want to know the cricket score. Or can't even use a faked-up tranny because it's not the place you use trannies. Like where he works, for instance. Province wouldn't let a man listen to Springbok during hours; private firm maybe, but not the province. So he's got to find a way of having himself an earplug and summat big enough for the works. What else can a man stuff in his ears? Carrots? I grant you. But another answer's that thing you brought round this morning. Makes sense, don't it?"

Too true it did. Kramer had to stop in the doorway to get his shoes on properly. Then he realized he needed a few more answers.

"You said the range of this thing was short—how short?"

"Size he had? Around ten, twenty feet. These private eyes lug around sets the size of an overnight bag if they are working at longer ranges."

"And the cost? Expensive you said?"

"Bleeding fortune; not your amateur's gear. Proper 007 stuff and then some."

"You're suggesting what? A foreign power would've had to foot the bill?" Kramer brought a chuckle into this.

"Aye, aye, that kind of shekels."

"Man, this is really something then? No bloody wonder . . ."

"What?"

"Forget it—forget all about it, Mr. Brighton," said Kramer, taking out twenty-five rand of his own money and tucking it into the limp fist.

Brighton held the money and the stare until his eyes began to glaze. Then he smiled, almost, and rolled over, giving a grunt of deep satisfaction.

"Never happened, Lieut. Now piss off."

The Widow Fourie looked up from the kitchen table, where she was setting down a bowl of chicken-noodle soup, three minutes from its packet.

"You didn't waste time," she said.

"Uhuh."

"Do it all by phone?"

"Uhuh."

"Then I'll just tell the kids they can talk now but must stay in their rooms—and you can let me hear the rest."

Kramer lifted the soup and placed it on the top of the washing machine. He had not been able to sit still in one place ever since leaving the fire station. He broke some bread, dunked it, and began spooning up nourishment. He was not an eating man, more of a refueler. And he paced about between each mouthful. Chewing crumbs.

"Give it a rest, Trompie! I'm going to go cross-eyed if you don't stop. Want mushrooms in your omelet?"

"Uhuh."

He took his last sup from the bowl as he plonked it into the sink, wiped an arm over his chin, and lit up.

"Really! Is it ulcers you want?"

"Uhuh."

"In your omelet?"

"Uhuh. What?"

"*Ach*, I might as well talk to the blinking wall sometimes. Never mind; have your think first."

She cracked four eggs and got busy.

"Like I said, Whipstock, he knew the number."

"Who, Trompie?"

"*Gazette* reporter, municipal and provincial, knows all departmental heads. Bloke called Cheyney is Swart's boss. Still celebrating, by the sound of it; called me 'old chap'—you know the kind. But I bulled the bugger good, oh, yes; he told me the lot. Enough anyway. Swart wasn't working on top classified stuff, but the three in the next office were mixed up in some road scheme with the Defense Force. Cheyney wouldn't say more, mad to blab anything on the phone, but, like I say, it was enough."

"Roads? They don't sound important. Do you want the mushrooms chopped fine?"

"Uhuh. Roads not important? With a coastline as long as this one? You're a—"

"Now, now."

"The point remains, my girl. Swart was right next door to secret information, okay?"

The Widow Fourie started to beat the eggs, chasing the bowl as it slid around the work top. Kramer held it for her.

"Point taken, sir."

"Now that priest was very interesting. You know what he said when I rang just now? I gave him my name and he says, 'Decided to come out in the open, have you?' "

"Hey?"

"So I say, what do you mean, Reverend? And he says, 'You've had your men outside my house for two days; didn't you think I knew?' "

"What could he mean?"

"Very, very interesting. Specially after I phoned Dan, the one who was in Security till he hurt his shoulder, owns that tearoom and a farm down near Drummond."

"It's ready now—mind the pan."

Kramer stepped aside to let her get by.

"Just casual like, I say to Dan, does he know a Catholic priest called Lawrence? I'm working on a case, see, and this priest seems a funny bugger to me. Made out I'd really phoned to ask if I can go shooting on his land sometime."

"And?"

"Old Dan laughs and says I must watch out—the priest is a red-hot Commy!"

"What did he mean?"

"*Ach*, the bugger must be some kind of liberal, but I would have heard myself if it had been more. Before now, that is. See?"

"Hand me that big fork, please, Trompie. Ta."

"But do you see? The pattern?"

"No; to be honest, I don't." She sighed, very content simply to be with her man.

"Jesus bloody Christ!" he exploded.

The Widow Fourie swung around, startled, outraged.

"Don't you dare shout at me like that!"

But Kramer seemed quite unaware of her response as he stood there, eyes tight shut. Unaware of anything—not even the burning tip of the Lucky Strike's stub as it sizzled down between his fingers, shriveling the hairs, blistering the skin. She had to knock it from his hand.

"Trompie?" she said.

His eyes opened.

"Trompie, what is it? Please tell me! *Please!"*

"Zondi . . ."

"I've never seen you so angry. Are you angry? What—"

"The bastards."

"No, don't do anything right now, Trompie. You mustn't. You were laughing before; I'll stop you going out."

The Widow Fourie barred the doorway.

"The pattern, my girl, the *real* pattern, just then, when I was talking."

Now Kramer's voice was so unnaturally soft she shivered. Shuddered right down the spine and backed away. Stopping again at the door to the hall, pressing it shut behind her.

"What—what are you going to do?"

"Ach, just make a couple of calls," he said lightly, and mean, lifting the telephone receiver.

"Who to?"

"A Kaffir doctor."

"Hey? And who else?"

"Colonel Muller, long distance; he's going to have to cut his holiday short."

"You're calling him back?"

"Uhuh."

"But why?"

"Because it's either that or I go into the murder business myself. Okay?"

thirteen

Zondi started to come around at six o'clock on the morning of December 27, and Dr. Mtembu was there to help him do it. His head still felt stuffed with thundercloud, and his cheek was burning, and his arm was aching, but never in years had he had such a good rest. He could sense as much throughout his spare frame, right down to the calluses on his soles, and for once hunger was his only discomfort. He had been relentless with that body. It was grateful.

It was also reluctant to get on the move again, and he needed assistance to reach the chair.

"Don't rush yourself," Mtembu advised. "You have been asleep two days, a very long time."

"Shabalala—where is he?"

"The prisoner?"

"Yes."

"Dead. He died in the car."

Zondi sighed, lilting the sound in the way of his people when they mourned.

"I went to much trouble to find him."

"Sit down. I will fetch some milk."

"Where is the nurse?"

"She is busy."

160

Zondi watched Mtembu slip out, puzzled. This was a strange business when a doctor ran errands for you. He hobbled over and drew aside the curtains surrounding his bed. There was one other patient in the small ward, inside a plastic tent, breathing like a rutting buck, but nobody else. He almost missed the chair getting back on it.

"For shame," he hissed at his body.

Remembering then, with a shudder, the women at his back and the sweat in his eyes as he ran. All for nothing. Or perhaps he had dreamed it in his long sleep. A nightmare.

Mtembu returned with the milk, and a plate of bread and butter besides.

"Eat as an old woman without teeth," he warned, "and drink like a sparrow."

"Am I farm boy, you speak to me thus?" Zondi snapped, pushing the glass away.

Mtembu laughed, too loudly, too anxious to be found a man of whimsical humor. There was fear in him and that, too, was strange.

"Answer me, Mr. Stethoscope."

"I apologize, Sergeant. I intended only to . . ."

"I have felt my head," said Zondi, continuing now in English, "and where is the wound that made me unconscious?"

"Shock to the general system, Sergeant."

That was a new one on Zondi, but another thought occurred to him.

"Why is it you wake me so early?"

"It is you who did the awakening."

"But why must I get up now?"

Again that curious glance away and flick of the tongue to keep the lips wet.

"Because your superior asked for you to join him whenever possible." Zondi rose unsteadily.

"Why didn't you say that straightaway? Get me my clothes."

Mtembu pointed to them on the locker.

"Shall I help you, Sergeant?"

"Ring for a police car."

"Your superior will come for you."

"He said this?"

"To myself, personally."

"Then ring him—*checha!*"

Mtembu hurried, all right, compounding Zondi's shaky bewilderment. This was not the world as he had left it.

By the time Colonel Muller had dropped off the family and reached CID headquarters, everything was in the bag and Kramer waiting for him on the top step. Muller, still dressed casually in yellow polo shirt, khaki shorts, sandals, and blue socks, gave just a shake of the head and no greeting. Kramer turned and led the way. Up the stairs and down the corridor. Outer door, inner door, rum tum tum, halt.

They talked for forty minutes.

Then Muller left his seat on the corner of the big desk under the Prime Minister's portrait, and walked the feeling back into one leg. He broke off his third circuit of the desk to sit down and use the internal line.

"Switch? Muller. I want you to ring Colonel Du Plessis and ask him to come to HQ quick as. And Lieutenant Scott. Are they? Good. Then I want you to find out for me if Brigadier Willems can be contacted at BOSS, Pretoria. *BOSS*—Bureau of State Security, you baboon! Not Boss Anybody! God in heaven, who am I speaking to? De Kok? Might have bloody guessed. Get on with it."

Kramer took the chair pointed out to him; caught and lit the small cheroot tossed across. He was enjoying all this.

"Tromp."

"Sir?"

"I intend taking this matter all the way," said Muller, holding his smoke.

"Uhuh."

Muller exhaled to avoid choking.

"Min-ister. Pardon. To the Minister himself."

"Hell."

"Hell, nothing! I'm not having anybody play silly buggers with my men's time! Bloody cheek!"

There was nothing Kramer could usefully add. He had said it all already, with maximum effect. So he simply nodded a few times.

"I mean, Tromp, it would have been different if they'd asked for our cooperation. Quite different. But to treat us as though we can't be trusted—that I will not have! Huh! What do they think *we* are? Russia-trained spies?"

"No, sir, just not so special as they are. We're dog-license cops."

"Bastards."

The internal telephone bleeped.

"Muller. What gives? Then get me his home number. Of course it isn't in the book, you—"

He slammed down the receiver again.

"Waste of breath. If that man's brains were dynamite, they wouldn't blow his bloody head off. And the same for some others we know."

"The thing that gets me," said Kramer, "is that you'd think chucking Swart in solitary would have been enough—hundred and eighty days to change his ways and come across."

"They must have been in a hurry then. Or have wanted to properly frighten the rest off. It was nice, though, you've got to admit: the public will always suspect the coon, but Swart's friends would know that a liberal like him isn't going to be carved up by his own kitchen boy. You said he spoiled the Bantu Shabalala?"

"Well, he didn't make him wait on the table longer than eight or something."

"There you are, you see? Pampered coons don't do things like this. Deterrent, bait—call it what you like, the idea was good."

Kramer reserved opinion. In his reckoning, the affair had all the hallmarks of the bumbling Du Plessis. God, it had been a shock to realize that the man had not been succeeded by Muller because of his own incompetence, but must have moved up in the world. Right to the top, in fact: security. State security, which, as every cadet learned, was the most important aspect of police work. Again, the mind boggled.

Bleep.

"On their way? Ta, De Kok. Now I don't want any interruptions—understood? Hey? No, she won't be."

Muller kept the receiver in his hand after the line went dead, testing its weight as though assessing its possibilities as a blunt weapon—his mood was very nasty. Then he snapped out of it and dropped the thing with a thud, chipping off a piece of plastic. His phone was a mess.

"Here goes, Tromp. Now you just leave the talking to me. Okay?"

"Pleased to, sir."

A double knock and, without waiting, Du Plessis poked his head around the door.

"Morning! What's the panic? Missed my kidneys on toast."

"Come in, please," said Muller.

Du Plessis raised his brows to Scott and the two of them entered the office, taking seats without invitation. Then Muller stood up, very tall against the high window, and his face difficult to see because of the light.

"I know what," said Scott. "There have been some sudden developments. Right, Colonel Muller?"

"Quite so."

"Have to be in the Wallace case then," chimed in Du Plessis, the sort who would enjoy party games.

"No."

"But it *can't* be the Swart!" Du Plessis said.

"It is."

"Involving who?"

Muller flipped another cheroot to Kramer and lit the last of the packet. His actions owed less to histrionics than they did to a full appreciation of an irrevocable word he was about to utter.

"You," he said. "Both of you."

Fools might have tried a laugh or two, a wink and slap on the back; it was sobering to observe how well Du Plessis and Scott controlled their responses. One went yellow and one white, but neither said anything. It was a silence to be measured in heartbeats, to be felt pressing on the eardrum, to be endured. It lasted a very long time.

Then Du Plessis stirred, reaching into his hip pocket for a white handkerchief. He used it delicately on his nose and then for jaunty display in his shirt pocket.

"Colonel Scott? Would you like to say anything to this gentleman?"

Colonel next! How the plot thickened. Muller and Kramer concurred in this, wordlessly.

"All I have to say," said Scott politely, "is to ask you to explain yourself, Colonel Muller. I'm sure you would not make such a statement without arming yourself with a suitable allegation."

Muller might have wavered at this moment, had Scott not missed out on the obvious question as to the nature of the involvement, and so made their complicity implicit.

"Would you deny," began Muller, discarding the cheroot, "that on the night of December the twenty-third, you deliberately removed one of my officers, Lieutenant Tromp Kramer, here present, from the scene of a killing in Skaapvlei? That you did not wish this officer to make his characteristically thorough investigation? That you wanted the murder treated as nothing more than a routine case involving a Bantu?"

"But how did we do this, Colonel?" asked Scott, a small smile at odds with a frown.

"Unfortunately for you, *Colonel*, there was not another murder in Trekkersburg that night," Muller continued, his voice steadier. "If there had been, perhaps this deception would never have come to light. But you had no murder. You had to settle for *any* violent death, and then, by throwing suspicion on the circumstances of this death, make it seem worthy of the lieutenant's attention. What the English call sending a man on a wild-goose chase? Am I right?"

"The boy Zondi remained on the case," Du Plessis said.

"Exactly, the boy Zondi. A Bantu. A Kaffir who would do what he was told."

Du Plessis looked across at Scott. They read off the same message in each other's eyes and shrugged.

"We deny nothing of this," said Scott.

And Muller gasped, despite himself.

When Zondi heard that plans had changed and he was to take a taxi, he took it first to Kwela Village, where Miriam and the children were pleased to see him alive. He showed them the cast on his arm, and they showed him the unwanted books that white youngsters had donated to

165

their school's Christmas tree. Then he had a big mug of tea with his wife, and told her what he remembered of the accident. She took up the story at Peacevale Hospital, giving him a full description of the morning she had been called to his bedside, and of the visit paid to her by the lieutenant. He left almost immediately, waiting only long enough to change into his other shirt and a clean pair of slacks.

Now, back in the office unofficially shared with Kramer, Zondi paced it restlessly, impatient to learn what was going on. But the duty man down at the entrance had told him that the lieutenant was in conference with Colonel Muller and could not be disturbed. This conference had been in progress for over an hour so probably he should not have long to wait.

Zondi looked at his watch again and put it to his ear to make sure it was still ticking. Shockproof, as the Indian trader had assured him.

But Zondi could tolerate only so much inactivity and then got a gut ache. So he sat himself down in his corner with two dockets taken off the lieutenant's desk. One had to do with Boss Swart; the other— astonishingly—with a man called Wallace, who had died in a motor accident.

The Swart docket was almost empty. It contained a few quite unremarkable photographs of the murder scene, plus forms filled in by Fingerprints, the laboratory, and Dr. Strydom. No statements, no list of suspects, nothing to engage the mind. But Zondi read every word all the same.

Then, after another look at his watch, he opened the Wallace docket. The first page had been prepared by the Traffic section, and was all very straightforward: race, name, age, address, occupation, time, manner, place, measurements, observations, and assessment. Several statements, also prepared by Traffic, followed this, giving the time of the accident in the estimation of residents who had heard the crash. The postmortem findings were mundane. The photographs were just that. So far so boring. Next came a small surprise: a report on the car by Fingerprints —negative, as it happened, but an extraordinary procedure all the same. Zondi wondered why the lieutenant had bothered to request such a thing—and, indeed, why he was bothering at all with such a matter. The equally unexpected laboratory report that followed was also an enigma for, apart from grouping the blood, giving the high alcohol level, and making a faintly sarcastic remark about glass fragments, it said nothing. But most astounding was a preliminary report by the lieutenant, a man not given to paper work, based on an interview with a colleague of the deceased: three whole pages describing how Wallace had arrived at the Old Comrades' Club and drunk far too much. This was dated December 24. All in all, what looked like a fine waste of time. Colonel Du Plessis.

He carried the dockets back to the other desk and put them side by side just as he had found them. Then he used one of his skeleton keys on the middle drawer, helped himself to a Lucky Strike, and locked it again. His first three puffs in days made him very dizzy and he had to sit down right where he was, in the lieutenant's chair. Which put a different perspective on things, and he saw what was happening and how he could make himself useful instead of just hanging about.

Because of his arm, he had first to find a driver, but was soon on his way out to Skaapvlei with the pictures.

The shoe was on the other foot now, and poised for a kick into Kramer's ribs.

"Man, I must say it was ingenious," remarked Scott, accepting a cheroot from the fresh pack Muller had produced.

"Yes, Tromp, always said you were one of my best," agreed Du Plessis, "only inclined to go off half cocked."

Kramer stood up, angry.

"First you say you don't deny taking me off the Swart case, don't deny God knows what else; now you tell the Colonel that we've got it all wrong. How's that?"

"Easy, man, easy," said Muller, motioning Kramer to be seated again. He had got right to the end of the accusation before the security man laughed in his face. It had hurt and confused him.

"The funny thing is," Scott went on, smug as ever, "that only last night Colonel Du Plessis actually suggested maybe we should come to you for the use of your special talents."

"Hey?"

"What is going on?" asked Muller, advancing a stage to exasperation. "Just tell me that, Colonel Scott! Explain how these facts don't add up."

"And they are *facts,*" stressed Kramer.

"I don't deny that either," Scott said, "just as your nose is a fact. But you go down to that fun fair place on Durban beachfront and look in the mirrors there. What happens? You can see your nose, and your eyes and your mouth and your chin, but they're all twisted out of shape. Same thing happened when you held up these facts."

"Thanks." Patronizing bastard.

The internal line bleeped and Muller quickly answered it.

"What? Oh, that? No, don't trouble—I don't want it anymore."

Scott looked amused, as if he knew what the Pretoria call had been about. He went over to fetch an ashtray from the windowsill, and remained there, slightly behind Muller, making him very uncomfortable.

"The thing that has impressed me," said Scott, "was how often you were right, Lieutenant—only you kept coming to the wrong conclusions. Would you admit to some sort of personal prejudice toward either Colonel Du Plessis or myself? Something that could affect your excellent judgment?"

Kramer made no response whatever.

"I see; well, then, my guess was a good one. When you had your suspicions aroused by my lack of a tan that morning in the swimming bath—an oversight which embarrasses me, but it had been very hot— you quite rightly decided I was not the person I claimed to be. But then you went on to assume that Colonel Du Plessis and I could only be engaged on something shady; you ruled out any idea of our motives being good ones. Your first mistake and the one which colored all the rest. You felt that in some way you were being exploited, and decided to find out how. Frankly we never thought there would be any contact between you and the Bantu woman Miriam Zondi, and yet our motives again were good. You were right—and here I think you did a first-class job—in the deductions you made about the hearing aid, but very wrong in your conclusions."

"All bluff and bullshit," said Kramer, unmoved. "What do you say, Colonel? Is this an explanation?"

He looked hard at Muller, who looked hard at his ankles.

"*Ach*, may as well tell them," said Scott to Du Plessis. "Got nothing to lose now."

And he came back to his chair and gave Du Plessis a nod to begin.

"Well, Tromp, my old friend, I'm sorry to find you would think so badly of me," said Du Plessis. "Your theory is that we waited until Colonel Muller took his Christmas holiday so that we could bump off a subversive passing secrets to a priest with leftist tendencies. You regard this—um—assassination? as a deterrent and possibly a way of flushing out a few others in the long grass. And you're angry because you were not let into the secret, but made to waste your time—and your boy's time—chasing wild ducks. Now that isn't nice, man, not from an old mate. But I suppose you pay me a compliment."

"What's that?"

"I'm not in security work, not in the slightest. Wish I was."

"Hey?"

"And of course you went the other way with poor old Swart, making out he was a bad bugger working for a foreign power even."

"He wasn't? Then where'd he get a special radio like that one?"

"From us," said Scott simply.

Which put a very different complexion on things, and on Colonel Muller in particular. The unhappy man sank back and swiveled his chair so that he need not meet anybody's eyes. While Kramer experienced a sensation first felt as a child when making his maiden journey in a fast lift, downward. His stomach came back off his diaphragm and bounced on his intestines. Just the once, however.

"Almighty God!" he said. "But that was still no reason."

"Ah, let me explain first, Tromp, let me explain. Go back to the night of the twenty-third. A message comes in that the body of one presumed to be Hugo Swart has been found stabbed in his kitchen. Murder Squad is immediately informed and Colonel Muller puts you on to it. Right? I come on at ten and find Colonel Scott here waiting in my office—this office, in fact. He identifies himself and then explains the position. This man Swart is a special agent of his department. Maybe you can explain this part better, John?"

Scott forsook his smoke rings.

"As you've already heard, Kramer, this priest Lawrence had himself a bad reputation for his carryings on. Just how far they went was becoming of some interest to us, so we fixed up for Swart to move into the parish and see what gives. He was already working as a draftsman for the province and in that department because of his good security rating."

"Don't rub it in, John!" chuckled Du Plessis, hoping he would. But it was an act of overfamiliarity which did him no good: the quick glare must have singed his eyelashes.

"As I was saying, we moved Swart in. The man's mother had been a Catholic and made him go to Mass till he was fifteen, so he knew what to do. Very soon he had worked his way in at Our Lady's, but nothing to report. His contacts on our side pushed him hard, but nothing. Then one meeting he says he has noticed something; many of the people coming to confession are from outside the district."

"Hell, it's common practice," interrupted Kramer. "Shows what a nonsense it is."

"Nobody's arguing, Lieutenant, but it was a good point. From how far *outside* the district were they coming? That's one question you can ask. Then remember Swart had been nearly living in this priest's pocket, knew all his moves, his timetable, but had not seen him engage in any suspicious activity—no secret get-togethers."

"The confession box?"

"Ah, you can be flexible then. Naturally we were interested in this little theory. Particularly as the confessional at Our Lady's was built into one side and completely soundproof. Sightproof, too; ideal for passing messages, even documents."

"But a priest wouldn't do a thing like that," Muller objected. "They take vows."

"And get funny ideas, too, Colonel," Scott replied. "They often imagine that God turns a blind eye if what they do is done in His name

—what about that saboteur the other day? It depends on how you read your Bible, not so?"

Müller mumbled an apology.

"I've got it," said Kramer. "Church is also a place where you can't listen to the radio!"

"Exactly—which is what I mean by how often you were right, Lieutenant. We had to think up an idea and our resident genius thought of the hearing aid. First we got Swart to complain to his fellow churchgoers about his ears, then we gave him the equipment. There is a little shelf in the confessional under the wire netting where he put the transmitter. It was a very special one, costing a lot, so as to pick up even the rustle of papers if necessary, because we couldn't get a camera in there. I see from Colonel Müller's face that he is still not happy about this arrangement, but tell me, what harm could come to the priest if he was doing his business honestly?"

"Oh, no, you're getting me wrong," Müller replied hastily.

"Fine. So what happened was this. For a whole month Swart listens in and hears nothing he shouldn't hear. I got on to his Trekkersburg contacts and said maybe we were wasting time and money—Swart did very nicely out of it, I can tell you. They went to see him and to pass on my doubts. Then, just one day later, he comes through with a piece of information. Man, that was luck for you."

"Can you say what it was?"

"Just a small mention that made us interested. Nothing by itself, but —well, you know. So we tell him to keep at it. All this stuff is very vague but some times up with what we already knew. We didn't take any action because this would probably spoil our chances of something really useful."

"How did he identify these callers?"

"That was the big problem. At the start, he just followed them out —this gave us a description: some were white, some were black. Then he intended to get the number of the vehicle they used. But these bastards were smart; they left on foot or were picked up down the road, too far for a clear sight of their plates."

"Didn't you put a man outside?"

"Sometimes we did, more recently. We didn't have enough personnel for a constant check, you see—we've always got a lot on our plate. The bugger of it was that only twice did we have a man in front when a suspect left."

"And you traced the numbers?"

"Yes, but did nothing with the ones my men took. A few that Swart thought would be worth it—earlier, that is—we checked out."

"Were they?"

"No, all honest citizens. Just as well we did not approach them direct. We got the dope, passed it on to him, and he tried the names in a round-about way on the priest. No reaction. We had a look at them, too, but nothing."

"This was the weakness of your method then—identification?"

"Only while the investigation stayed low priority. When Swart came through with something much stronger last week, I moved two men in for all the time confessions were held. But the priest's friends must have picked up their Volksy the first night because Swart heard nothing more."

"They could have picked up *Swart*, Colonel."

"Yes, that is the line we have been taking. But I'm buggered if I see how."

"What I can't understand is why you haven't hauled the priest in, chucked him in solitary," Kramer persisted.

"That's just the background. Dupe here will tell you the rest."

For once Kramer was only too eager to hear what the old bitch had to say.

"Right, I'll do my best. *Ach*, you see, this development put me in a bit of a spot. If you hadn't already gone out to Skaapvlei, Tromp, there would have been no problem. The thing was, the Colonel here didn't want a good detective on the job."

"*Jesus . . .*"

"No, honestly, man, that was the position. You could have spoiled the whole thing by poking your nose into it and then asking questions that would be like lifting up a stone—you would scatter everything hiding under it."

172

"You see," cut in Scott, "straightaway I realized the best move was in point of fact to treat it like an ordinary murder. This would confuse the bastards and the chances were that one or other of them would get in contact with the priest. For all they knew, perhaps, it could have been a mistake killing Swart. They would want to talk it over."

"Men of conscience, remember," sneered Du Plessis.

"Go on," said Scott.

"Well, I had to get you away from Swart, didn't I, Tromp? And as you correctly guessed, I had to find something else and the car crash was all I had. I apologize now but, as you will see, it was for the best."

"Uhuh."

"Zondi we kept because Shabalala could always be the scapegoat until we got our proper man."

"You were confident he would find him?"

"Naturally. Probably quicker than we could, and more easily. We kept an eye on him, of course."

"Of course."

"To get on with what happened, after you left for the car crash, we —that is the Colonel and his men—brought in the two suspects whose numbers had been noted by the man outside the church. We got nothing out of them. They denied any knowledge of any political conversations or connections with the priest. The colored started to change his story this morning, mind you, but maybe he just wants to sleep."

"Look, let me wrap this thing up," Scott said, impatient with Du Plessis' oratory. "After the killing we checked every source of information—nothing. Right through the next day we watched the priest's house—nothing. We sent in a man to Mass but he reported all seemed normal. Man, this wasn't making sense. So I decided to put a bit of the pressure on; I got the blokes watching his place to come out into the open where he could see them. Still nothing."

"What about that 'strong' stuff Swart gave you last week? I take it that it included a name?"

"Yes, it did. She denies everything as well. Flatly. Every word. Tried to hang herself in the cells, though."

"Uhuh. And so?"

"Night before, I'd got one of my best Bantus to have another chat with Shabalala's town wife. She put him on to his cousin, and this man told us Shabalala had probably run off because his family was moving house. Seems a bloody-fool reason to us, but you know these wogs—irresponsible. Then on Christmas Eve I began to wonder if Shabalala didn't have something useful to tell me: if you looked at the times carefully, he could have been a witness. So I radioed my blokes keeping an eye on Zondi to ask how things were going. They said he was kicking up hell at Jabula—that it would be dangerous to go in without stens. Is he usually like this, Kramer?"

"Comes and goes."

"I see. So I ordered them to stick around—didn't want a big fuss, naturally—and see what happened. Just before midnight they come through: Zondi has suddenly appeared with his prisoner and driven off. Do they let him carry on down here or what? I tell them I want a few questions asked of Shabalala straightaway and, as Zondi hasn't got a radio, they'd better stop him on the road."

Kramer tightened his grip on the armrests, knuckles showing like bare bone. Muller leaned forward anxiously.

"Yes, I can see what's on your mind, Lieutenant, but I have it on oath my blokes didn't mean what happened. It was your Kaffir. He drove like a bloody madman when they came alongside. Frikkie was yelling at him who they were but he took no notice. Nearly killed all of them, Frikkie says. They even tried to slow down but— Look, you can ask him yourself."

"I will."

"Then, of course, I still wanted to know what Zondi had got out of Shabalala and I didn't want you to know because—well—Dupe here said it would become a very personal matter for you, and you'd get your nose in and do what he said with the stones. The sleep didn't hurt him."

"I'll ask that, too."

Scott was surprised by this remark—so much so, Kramer took another lift ride and cursed his big mouth. This was no way of scoring a point.

"That Kaffir," added Kramer, "does nothing but bloody sleep!"

It got its laugh of absolution.

"And we tell you all this," said Scott, with sudden weariness, "because on the twenty-seventh of December—that's today, two days later—we still haven't a bloody clue who did it. We're just going to have to pull in that priest after all, spoil our chances of more."

"Uhuh. But what about that thing you took from the study? Something did disappear and you haven't said what."

"*Ach*, it was just this," said Scott, handing over a worn Missal that he took from his briefcase.

Kramer flicked through its dog-eared pages, stopping at a few numbers written faintly in pencil over a feast-day litany.

"Car numbers—the ones I told you about earlier, Tromp. All Trekkersburg, all harmless. Swart used this book for taking his notes in the church—you can see some pages with conversation on them—all stuff we'd had before, so don't read it. What we've been working on is up near the front."

"Chemicals" was the word Kramer found there, written in Afrikaans.

"Explosives?" he ventured.

"What else, man? Only it's new, you see. Swart said there had been talk of explosives between the priest and a man who was going to find out what ingredients were available from over the border. But he never got round to reporting they actually discussed the chemicals."

"Then they might have deliberately brought up the subject to see if he reacted—they must have found the bug."

"My thoughts exactly, Tromp—and this happened the night he was murdered."

"Hmmm," said Kramer, a thought later.

"Some doubt, Lieutenant?"

"No; I suppose he could have jotted it down *after* leaving the church —otherwise they would have taken the book. The priest, for example, had all the time he needed in the house before ringing us."

"You know what?" said Scott. "Bugger all this clever stuff. Let's have this bastard Father Lawrence in here and give him the once-over. A bird in the hand, as the English say—hey, Colonel Muller?"

Scott left abruptly, Du Plessis on his heels.

Then Kramer rose, walked slowly over to stand before the desk, stiffened up, and lifted his chin.

"Sorry, sir," he said, after a pause.

"From you, I suppose that's really something," Colonel Muller replied. "But get the hell out of my sight."

fourteen

The greatest hurt of them all, far crueler than anything else suffered on Kramer's rack of regret, was what this fiasco must have done to the Widow Fourie. She had forgiven and forgotten, returned, come back at Christmas, the best present he ever unwrapped, and such had been her welcome. Two hours of tentative happiness, and then God knew how many more of worry and anguish, of sick concern for the brats of a Kaffir as willful, stupid, and deaf to bloody reason as himself. Yes, Zondi shared some of the blame, but only some. The rest fell entirely on Kramer. Went off half cocked, Du Plessis had said. Distracted by prejudice, Scott had said. They were right, the bastards. No, not bastards; not this time round.

Jesus, what a clown he had been that morning when the message about the train came through. He could have dropped everything right then and sod the lot of them. It would not have been the first time he had told Du Plessis to go stick a report in a pigeon's hole. And all Scott had wanted was him out of the way, so it would not have mattered anyhow. But no; pride, conceit, arrogance—give it what fancy name you liked—had got the better of him. Made him go racing around putting two and two together and getting twenty-two on his slate. Bloody wonderful. If he had just approached Scott at the swimming pool, the chances were he would have been put in the picture, had the rest of the day and the next with the kids and herself. Started again, differently, so it would last, so she would never go away again. Oh, Christ.

He reached out again to dial the flat but found he still could not bring himself to do so. There might be no answer. Again.

The phone tinkled and never got the chance to ring properly.

"Yes? Look—"

"Old McDonald here, Lieutenant. That is you, isn't it?"

Kramer moved to replace the receiver, then decided to get it over with.

"Kramer speaking, Mr. McDonald. I was going to give you a ring actually, tell you that we've dropped the case."

"Oh, I see."

"Yes, nothing to it—never thought there would be. But we've got to be certain in these matters."

"It was just—"

"Uhuh?"

"First day back, Lieutenant, getting down to the hard graft again, tidying up. Naturally I started with my late colleague's affairs. Something very distressing—very odd."

"In what way?"

"Well, it amounts to this: Mark surrendered all his policies a week ago."

"Hey?"

"Cashed them in; did it on the quiet, too, somehow. Twenty thousand rand in all."

"*Twenty*, you said?"

"Yes, quite a bundle that would make."

"But what the hell did he do with it?"

"It isn't in his bank—I've made discreet inquiries—and his wife hasn't seen a penny of it."

"You've been on to her?"

"Had to; there was a call from head office about his using the firm's car—you know what head offices are like, no blooming sense or compassion. I hoped she'd say theirs was out of commission that night, but it wasn't. But they simply *can't* claim any off the estate, not with the way it is now."

"Forget the car—tell me more about this money. How was he paid?"

"By transfer. The bank— Look, don't tell anyone about this, please; more than my friend's job is worth."

"Talk, Mr. McDonald. No pack drill."

"Mark withdrew this money in *cash*—small notes."

"And nobody was told why?"

"My friend couldn't very well ask around this morning, could he? But he did remember one teller saying that the nice Mr. Wallace had his secret vices after all."

"Such as?"

"Gambling. He'd said he needed it for gambling debts—a man who wouldn't even take a jackpot ticket with the rest of us on a Saturday. And horses are one thing, the sort of gambling he tried to imply was another."

"Man, oh, man."

"Yes, Lieutenant, just how I feel."

They both listened to the background noises on the line for a while. Then Kramer flipped open his notebook.

"Remember he said he wanted to talk to you that night at the Comrades' Club, Mr. McDonald? Could it have been about this?"

"It's been on my mind ever since—this isn't the first time I've tried to get you."

"I'm sorry, Mr. McDonald. Another case, a big one. Although this sounds . . ."

"Yes, Lieutenant?"

"A big one, too, man. Now I want you to say nothing about this, understand? I'll be round soon as I can so you can show me the papers. Okay?"

"I'll be here."

Kramer killed the call with a push on the cradle bar, flipped on three pages in his notebook, found an address, found a number in the directory, and dialed it.

"Good morning, madam. This is the police here, CID. Can you tell me if Miss Samantha Simon is there, please?"

"Oh, no. I'm sorry. She's gone to work."

"When did she leave?"

"Let me think. A bit earlier than usual, I suppose—about eight. Yes, just after her breakfast. The ten-past bus."

"Do you take a paper, madam?"

"Pardon?"

"The *Trekkersburg Gazette*—do you have it delivered?"

"Oh, yes."

"Did Miss Simon see a copy of it by any chance?"

"My hubby and me always let her have it first. We're retired, you see. We have all day."

"Uhuh. And when she went out, did she have anything with her? A suitcase maybe?"

"Pardon?"

"Was she carrying anything, madam?"

"Oh, no, just her handbag."

"Thanks and bye," Kramer said, again prodding the cradle bar.

The number rang for some time before being answered.

"Librarian speaking," said what sounded like an answering machine.

"Oh, good morning. I'm sorry to trouble you like this, but you see I've found this season ticket—bus season, that is—and it's got your address on it."

"Well?"

"I was wondering if I could speak to the person it belongs to, Samantha Simon?"

"Miss Simon? Busy at the counter."

"She is the pretty one, isn't she?" Kramer leered audibly.

"So that's your game!"

The librarian slammed down his receiver and left Kramer quite certain that nothing would be said to alarm the cool little bitch until he got to her.

Yes, cool was the word for it. She must have realized that now the man was dead his finances would show a deficit that would bring her back into the action. Yet to have cut and run would have been her downfall. She was going to bluff this one out, and had probably taken a few precautions as it was. He would enjoy seeing how long she stayed cool in the heat of what he planned to do.

Just at that moment, as Kramer was grabbing up the spare cuffs, Zondi entered the room holding his nose with his good hand.

"You, you bugger! Where have you been?"

"*Hau!*" replied Zondi. "Since when has the boss been doing the rubbish collection?"

"What the hell do you mean?"

"The Chev, in the boot, rubbish to the top and a smell that is terrible."

Kramer bloody nearly hit him. And it had been for his sake, too, the Widow had gone to such trouble. Instead he shouldered Zondi out of the way roughly, perversely pleased to hear the thump of plaster cast against the filing cabinet. Then he plunged into three startled Africans just outside the door.

"Jesus!" shouted Kramer. "What the bloody Christ next? What do you want here, *slima?*"

The Zulu obscenity slammed into the trio as hard as he would have liked to place his boot.

"They want nothing here," said Zondi from the door, rubbing his shoulder. "It is *I* who want *them*. And you, too, boss, for they are witnesses."

"To what?" Kramer asked over his shoulder, striding away.

"The Swart case, of course, boss. They all saw the white master who you think did it."

Kramer and Zondi left the servants with the Bantu detective constable who had done the driving, and was now to take down detailed statements from all three. They went back into the office and closed the door.

"Nice work," Kramer said, indicating that Zondi should draw his stool up to the desk.

"Thank you, boss. You were waiting for me that you did not ask these people before?"

"Something of the kind. Cigarette?"

He unlocked his middle drawer, lit two Luckies, and handed one across.

"But tell me, Zondi—how was it you moved so fast this morning? I wasn't here to fill you in on the case."

Zondi stubbed out his Lucky, shuddering.

"I come here, there is nobody to greet me. So I have a little look at these dockets. I read them and wonder why my boss is worrying himself with this Traffic case. I put the dockets back like I find them and, *hau*, see the truth of the matter."

"What do you mean exactly?"

"The way the dockets are side by side—the boss is taking the cases together. Very, very clever, the nose blood."

"Hey? You just tell me how your thinking went—I'm interested."

Flattery was Zondi's Achilles' leg, bugger one tendon.

"Like this, boss. When the man Wallace goes to the drinking place, he tells the people there that it is so hot that his nose has been bleeding and they see little bit of blood on his shirt and are sorry for him."

"Uhuh."

"Now the laboratory, boss: I see this work was done down in Durban because ours was closed for Christmas. You send the clothes, blood sample, say analyze, and they don't see anything strange they should ring you up about."

"No?"

"*Ikona*, because many times the men at the wheel in vehicles have blood from passengers on them."

"Wallace didn't have a passenger—did he?"

"Ah, yes, boss, but did you tell the laboratory this? See, you cannot trick me. They get just the one shirt, the one suit, the one form with one name on it. It is alcohol you are really interested in. They tell you it is high. Then they test quickly the blood stains, thinking you are mad maybe, and put down O group and A group. Wallace is O group, am I right?"

"No cheek, now."

"And Boss Swart is A group—the small quantity, simple! Then this glass they make jokes about—that, too, I can understand."

Kramer, who had taken the report out of the envelope that morning, just before Muller was due to arrive, without more than a glance at the alcohol level, now gave it his undivided attention.

The technician had written: "Glass fragments in left trouser turn-up, from lead content possibly Venetian origin. What was he doing in his motor, running a bar?"

Hell, Kramer had actually read the words "glass fragments," come to think of it, but had got no further because the appalling scribble irritated him in his haste. He had also seen it as "glass" in its general sense, expecting pedantry about windshields, and not in the sense of "*a* glass," or he would have never skipped the rest. The truth was, and it was best kept to himself, his only reason for looking at the thing at all had been to see if the lab had agreed to play ball in hammering Du Plessis. He had told them it was only an exercise for the hell of it, a favor he would explain later.

"And that was why you took these pictures out to Skaapvlei?" Kramer said, spreading out the selection showing Mark Wallace and his firm's wrecked car.

"It seemed what I could do for you, boss. The two women, they both saw this car near the house on the night he was stabbed. They were sitting by the gutter near to where it was left. They also saw the master go into the house and come out after the other master came home. They saw he had a bad chest; his lungs made sounds like an old dog."

"Catarrh," said Kramer after a quick look at Strydom's post-mortem report.

"I did not know the meaning when I saw it, boss."

"You're forgiven. But why didn't these women come forward?"

"They thought it was Shabalala who killed him, boss. This is what everyone was thinking; the policeman had said so."

Damn Van der Poel and his pimp's bloody soul; his chatter and preconceptions had screwed the case right at the start.

"What about the man you brought in?"

"A friend of the man Shabalala, who works on the other side of the road. He gets off at seven and sometimes he went in to help with the washing up so it was finished quickly."

"Oh, yes?"

"He can swear that Shabalala put the key under a brick by the back door when he left the house after work."

"Did Swart know this?"

"How can I tell, boss? But it is what many servants do, for their masters do not like to trust them with a key, not so?"

Kramer was familiar with this commonplace of crazy logic and could only be mildly surprised that Swart subscribed to it. Probably he had just never checked on a habit Shabalala had picked up elsewhere. Many householders failed to make the most elementary checks on the security of their homes. Often the worst offenders, in this respect, were single persons, like Swart, who thought they had nothing to lose.

But this was going off at a tangent.

"And now tell me, Zondi," said Kramer, noting the time, "what was it Shabalala told you about that you wouldn't tell Miriam?"

"*Hau*, Boss, two very strange things!"

"Go on."

"First there is this blue VW that tries to kill me! Two friends of the boss Swart, Shabalala says. He—"

"But what else?"

"Shabalala had a mad job sometimes, boss. His master makes him go to the boots of cars that are parked in the street and take from them parcels."

"Parcels? What of?"

"That he did not know—but they were very light weight, like paper."

Kramer ran all the way.

The head librarian tried to interfere but was thrust aside by two words, one of which he never allowed in any book on his shelves. Kramer did, however, say it very softly and disturbed no one else; not even the unwholesome old man casting an eye over the seductive covers New Fiction had to offer. As for Samantha Simon, she turned merely at the sound of his voice.

"You?"

"Me. Another little chat, please. Okay?"

She took a step toward him, faltering.

"Here?"

The girl who faced him now was very different from the defiant little miss last confronted in the tearoom. Her face was the color of mealie porridge, and her eyes as lusterless as farm eggs. While her mouth, her most attractive feature before, was slack, ugly, awkward with words, as though the effect of a dentist's injection had yet to wear off. Certainly it all had to do with the deadening of pain.

"No, Miss Simon. I think up on the gallery would be more private."

For an instant something flashed in those pinked eyes, then, with a shrug, she started for the staircase. The ascent was excruciatingly slow until about halfway up, when she began taking the steps two at a time. Kramer hurried after her and was at her side when she broke down.

"No need to talk actually," he said, handing her a khaki handkerchief, then daring an arm around her shoulders. "Just show me where it was that Mark was standing when he said he saw a man watching you two. It's for his sake I ask you. Honest."

Samantha moved to the spot without a word, then reined in her sobs with one great heaving breath.

"There," she said, pointing.

The label on the nearest bookcase bore the legend CHEMISTRY— which, in hasty translation into Afrikaans, could easily emerge as "chemicals." Kramer had trouble with his own breathing as he crouched to examine the underside of the shelf at waist height. Yet there they were: three small punctured holes. Not woodworm, or even bookworm, but the mark of that truly uncommon species, the three-legged bug.

All the brass—Scott, Du Plessis, and Muller—turned up at the mortuary at five sharp that evening for Samantha Simon's identification of the body.

"*Ach*, sorry, but she's not here yet," Kramer apologized, arriving at ten past and finding them gathered expectantly in the small hallway. "Zondi will be bringing her down when she's ready."

Or, to be precise, Zondi would be bringing her down when the Widow Fourie decided the girl was ready—but he kept this to himself. Going around to the flat had been pure bloody genius; the Widow Fourie had taken Samantha under her wing immediately and sent Kramer packing, just as he had hoped. Which freed him, of course, to make a number of edifying calls, and to reach certain gratifying conclusions.

His elation showed.

"Out with it, man," snapped Scott, not amused at having been kept in the dark since lunchtime. "Where did you get with the car numbers from the Missal?"

"Far enough, sir—but I'd prefer to wait until we get a positive ident on Swart."

"Sod that for a start. My men checked out those car owners, not a single one even capable of being a subversive. I want to know what you found."

"Victims."

"Hey?"

"Blackmail victims."

"*All* of them?"

"Just the two, Wallace and a schoolteacher. But there must have been others, because he had about forty thousand stashed away under—"

"Just a minute," Scott interrupted. "You're not saying a bloke of mine was extorting funds?"

"Too right, Colonel. I'm sorry, but that's the way it was."

Du Plessis gasped, then turned a dangerous red.

"You'd better be able to explain an allegation like that, Lieutenant —and quickly!"

"Call it a supposition at this stage, Colonel, but I think you'll see I'm proved right by Miss Simon. It all fits."

"Just tell us," Muller urged him quietly.

This was different.

"Okay, sir, for what it's worth. Best we start right back when Swart first got mixed up in this church. You'll remember the Colonel here said the reports were negative, then Swart got the idea of putting a bug into the confessional. Very ingenious and an obvious weak spot. But did he get results straightaway, Colonel?"

Scott shook his head.

"No, a little time went by before the first report. Now think about those reports very carefully: they were all vague, the names in them were names well known to the public, never mind us blokes. And note, too, that when you hauled them in last night, they all denied any knowledge of what Swart had said about them."

"Well, so what?" Du Plessis asked scornfully. "It's just a matter of time."

"Sir, you think they are lying. I've got an idea that *Swart* was the liar. He lied because he had to keep Colonel Scott's lot happy or they'd have pulled him out of there—and out of his nice comfy house in Skaapvlei. Could be his first reports were just to keep him in business until he could think of a way of keeping up the good life."

"Christ," said Muller.

"Sir? You see what I'm driving at? All the time we've been overlooking the main point about that confession box. We've been thinking in terms of political secrets being the only secrets that might be heard in there. What about all the others? Maybe they couldn't threaten the fatherland but, to the people involved, they'd be enough to destroy their own lives if they got out. Little, sordid, disgraceful secrets—ah, but with something in common with the others, as far as Mr. Hugo Swart was concerned: cash value."

"Impossible," snorted Du Plessis.

"Not for an intelligent man," Kramer relished saying, "and Swart was intelligent, up to a point. The trouble was he didn't hear many secrets like this because, whatever your personal opinion, these were God-fearing folk he was eavesdropping on. But any group has a few deviants, buggers with personality problems they hate but can't get away from, and also a few blokes like Wallace, who fall off the straight and narrow. Who knows? Maybe Swart found up to a dozen in the congregation itself, and took them to the cleaner's. Then he had to look further afield. He comes across Wallace and a schoolteacher who is crazy for women's underwear."

"What's this?" Du Plessis asked. "Fact or more of your bloody fantasy?"

"Fact. He was one of the car owners on the list from the Missal. I interviewed the poor sod this afternoon and confirmed the pickup method using the hired car, et cetera. Also that Swart made his threats by phone."

"And the other car owners?"

"Swart used them for a cover-up."

"Used *us*, you mean!" flared Muller.

"Yes, sir, very cheeky, but an easy way of getting the names and addresses he wanted. He bargained on the Colonel's inquiries being discreet and purely political."

Scott still said nothing.

"This teacher had to sell his car to get enough to buy silence, you see, and then he was finished. But with Wallace, Swart saw he could probably do a lot better. I checked with Wallace's wife this afternoon, by the way. She says he 'lapsed' about the time I reckon Swart heard his sad little story."

"Which means, Tromp?"

"That he stopped going to church. The priest wouldn't help me on this, but he did agree that sometimes a man comes to him in a position like Wallace was in and expects to be told it's all right, very innocent, and he can carry on the good work. The priest also agreed he tells them it's not—they must give up the dolly right away. *And* he agreed that sometimes the man in question gets very angry and buggers off. Between the lines, I think he was giving us a hand there."

"Very nice. I'm with you," Muller said.

"Call it corny, if you like, but when a bloke thinks he's in love, he can be bloody stupid," Kramer said, mainly for Du Plessis' benefit. "But to get back to Swart: he phones Wallace and demands so much. Wallace hits such a panic, he gets that money to him right away—again a time factor you can check on later, through the insurance office's headquarters. Aha, thinks Swart, this could be worth a bit more."

"But why doesn't he give up the girl, Tromp? That would be only sensible."

"Why should he? He's finished with the church, the damage is done, and the blackmailer has promised to lay off. Everything in his world has gone very sick; the only good thing left is the girl. See what I mean? Personally, though, thinking about it now, I reckon that Wallace did intend chucking her—he talked to McDonald, his colleague, about it—but was trying to do it the nice way, slowly and gently and all that crap. But before this can happen, Swart decides to have another try. And to hit Wallace with maximum force, the best way is to use very personal information, to make him feel there's nowhere—"

"So he puts the bug into the library!" said Muller. "He puts the bug there and has another go. Careless, though, letting Wallace see him there."

"Perhaps, perhaps not. Wallace hadn't connected him then, of course. Anyway, Swart overhears their conversation and clobbers the poor sod again. This time, after he's paid up, Wallace gets rid of Samantha. Everything is going to be all right. I borrowed a library book from his place so I'd have—*ach*, never mind that—but I had another look at it this morning and got the date of their parting from it. This date was the same day as Wallace surrendered his other policy."

"How did he connect then, if that's what you're trying to say?"

"When Swart got too bloody clever and tried a third time. He sent Wallace a Christmas card and signed it "Samantha"—but he also underlined the word 'prosperous.' "

Du Plessis blinked.

"And so?"

"Well, this word had been used quite a lot by Samantha that time in the library when Swart was listening. It was a word that must have been ringing still in Wallace's ears. Before Swart had obviously been careful not to give away how he knew things, but this was a clear indication that a certain conversation had been overheard. I'd say Wallace remembered the man he saw, had his memory jogged by the Jesus on the card, remembered Swart from the church—he always sat near the confessional—and put two and two together. Maybe he even had his suspicions before—who knows?—but this did it. He had forked out everything he could, he had given up the girl, he had tried to get back to normal and then, right at Christmas, it all blows up again. Notice that 'prosperous' could also be a threat of more demands. Anyway, he takes his firm's car up to the church because it won't be recognized, follows—"

"Wouldn't he have to be in the house already?" Muller broke in.

"The priest helped me there again. Seems Swart went home to fetch something before the Mass; that's when Wallace must have tailed him. Wallace waited for him to push off, found the key in the obvious place under the brick, and went inside the house. What he had in mind then, we can't really say, but he must have been in one hell of a state. If murder was his plan, then you'd think he'd have taken a weapon. Anyway, Swart comes home and Wallace sees him in the kitchen with the radio on and the hearing aid off. Maybe they have a few words, who knows? Swart plays it cool, makes himself a drink, doesn't offer one to Wallace. Or maybe Wallace just goes bloody berserk at the sight of him, grabs up a knife from the table, and uggh!"

The three colonels exchanged a round of glances and then looked back at Kramer. Muller was impressed, Du Plessis bewildered, Scott inscrutable.

"When an ordinary, decent bloke like Wallace does a thing like this," Kramer said after a pause, "he can act very cool. The head shrinkers have a word for it—dissociated something or other. They kill and they walk away calmly; it isn't real for them. They can also want to tell somebody about what they have done—like that woman who reported killing her kids with plastic bags. Which is why I think that Wallace went to the Comrades' Club to see McDonald, only McDonald was too busy singing songs about bloody shepherds watching their flocks by night. So Wallace drank up and set off home, came to that corner, and thought what the hell—he knew, right inside, he was a dead man already."

This time the pause lasted some minutes. Then Scott finally broke his long silence.

"All I can say is that Swart's lucky *he* is a dead man, my friends, very lucky!"

"Hear, hear," growled Muller.

"The bastard! I gave him a position of trust and what does he do with it? Takes advantage of people at their weakest, exploits his—"

"She's here!" whispered Du Plessis.

They turned as one man. Samantha Simon, wearing dark glasses and smelling sweetly of gin, came through the screen door all on her own.

The mortuary sergeant, Van Rensburg, who had no doubt been doing a bit of eavesdropping himself, emerged from his office, harumphed, and' stepped forward with due solemnity.

"This way, please, miss. It won't take a second."

When Samantha reappeared, it was without her glasses. The eyes were bright again, bright and gleaming and horrible to look at.

Scott approached her, his manner very formal.

"Was that the man you saw in the library while you were in the company of Mark Clive Wallace?" he asked.

"Yes."

"You are certain of that, Miss Simon?"

"Yes."

"You would swear to it in a court of law?"

"Oh, God!" she choked. "Yes, yes, yes! It's him! The bastard who played gooseberry on us! Do you want it in blood?"

Then she fled between them before anyone had a chance to explain how necessary it was to be sure of things. The screen door clattered open and banged shut.

"Of course, there are still a few details—"

Scott spun on Du Plessis.

"Don't talk crap, man! If Swart was around, we'd have more than enough for a conviction!"

Du Plessis scowled peevishly.

"Well, I thought at least someone would thank me. After all, if I hadn't made the coincidence happen, then—"

"Coincidence? Is that what you call it? This morning it was a different story. Wallace's death was a *consequence*, you bloody idiot. The only coincidence was there wasn't another violent death that night—get it?"

Hurt deeply, Du Plessis slunk away to his proper place in bureaucratic obscurity. Muller tactfully led Van Rensburg into the office and closed the door, leaving Scott alone in the hallway with a very happy man.

"Ta," said Kramer, grinning.

"Tromp, it's me that should do the thanking, hey?" Scott replied. "My department is in your debt."

"BOSS?"

Scott gave an almost imperceptible shake of the head. Kramer knew then he had asked enough questions for one day. So, with a brief shake of hands, they parted.

And some minutes later, Zondi came in from the car park to find Kramer lost in thought.

"Go all right, boss?"

"Perfect."

"That is good."

"Oh, Colonel Scott asked me to thank you."

"What for, boss?"

"Put it this way," said Kramer, pushing him aside on his way out. "If it wasn't for you, Zondi, old son, then *quis pus custard et?*"

Other mysteries you'll enjoy from the Pantheon
International Crime series include:

Peter Dickinson   <u>King & Joker</u>   71600
<u>The Last Houseparty</u>   71601
<u>The Lively Dead</u>   73317
<u>The Poison Oracle</u>   71023

"Every new book of Dickinson's can be approached with anticipation."

—Newgate Callendar, *The New York Times Book Review*

Reginald Hill   <u>A Killing Kindness</u>   71060
<u>Who Guards the Prince?</u>   71337

"Hill's characters are clearly etched. The presence of a real writer makes itself felt."   —*The New York Times*

Norman Lewis   <u>Cuban Passage</u>   71420

"An unusually trim and plausible thriller."   —*The New Yorker*

Peter Lovesey   <u>The False Inspector Dew</u>   71338

"Irresistible...delightfully off-beat...wickedly clever."
—*Washington Post Book World*

James McClure   <u>The Blood of an Englishman</u>   71019
<u>The Caterpillar Cop</u>   71058
<u>The Gooseberry Fool</u>   71059
<u>The Steam Pig</u>   71021

"James McClure's are not only...first-rate procedurals, but they throw light on the human condition in the land of apartheid."
—*The New York Times*

William McIlvanney   <u>Laidlaw</u>   73338

"It has been a long time since I have read a first mystery as good as this one."   —Robin W. Winks, *The New Republic*

Poul Ørum   <u>Scapegoat</u>   71335

"Not only a very good mystery, but also a highly literate novel."
—*Maj Sjöwall*

Julian Rathbone   <u>The Euro-Killers</u>   71061

"Rathbone's new novel is quite exceptional...subtle yet straightforward and truthful."   —*Library Journal*

Per Wahlöö   <u>Murder on the Thirty-First Floor</u>   70840

"Something quite special and fascinating."
—*The New York Times*

See next page for coupon.

Look for the **Pantheon International Crime** series at your local bookstore or use this coupon to order. *All titles in the series are $2.95.*

Quantity	Catalog #	Price
_____	_____	_____
_____	_____	_____
_____	_____	_____
_____	_____	_____
_____	_____	_____
_____	_____	_____
_____	_____	_____
_____	_____	_____
_____	_____	_____
_____	_____	_____
_____	_____	_____

$1.00 basic charge for postage and handling $1.00
25¢ charge per additional book
Please include applicable sales tax

Total

Prices shown are publisher's suggested retail price. Any reseller is free to charge whatever price he wishes for books listed. Prices are subject to change without notice.

Send orders to: **Pantheon Books, PIC 15-2, 201 East 50th St., New York, NY 10022.**

Please send me the books I have listed above. I am enclosing $_____which includes a postage and handling charge of $1.00 for the first book and 25¢ for each additional book, plus applicable sales tax. Please send check or money order in U.S. dollars only. No cash or C.O.D.s accepted. Orders delivered in U.S. only. Please allow 4 weeks for delivery. This offer expires 5/31/84.

Name_____

Address_____

City_____State_____Zip_____